Hurricane Season

Hurricane Season

By

BJ Phillips

Desert Palm Press

Hurricane Season

By BJ Phillips

ISBN: 9781942976127
ISBN (epub): 9781942976134
ISBN (pdf): 9781942976141

Desert Palm Press
1961 Main Street, Suite 220
Watsonville, California 95076
www.desertpalmpress.com

Editor: Mary Hettel
Cover Design: Michelle Brodeur

Printed in the United States of America
First Edition — June 2016

Acknowledgement

First of all, I have to thank my family—my parents, my brother and sisters, and my daughter—for always believing that I would write a book. Someday. I just had to believe in myself. My mom always said it's never too late to do what you want. She was right. Thanks, Mom.
I don't think I could've done this without my favorite author (and now friend), AJ Adaire. As my first beta reader, you saw something worth saving when you volunteered to read this manuscript over two years ago. You've encouraged me to keep working on it all this time, becoming a good friend as well as mentor. I appreciate all the hours we've spent together discussing writing and life in general.

In 2014, I heard about something new called the Golden Crown Literary Society Writing Academy. The year-long Writing Academy literally changed my life, and I started thinking of myself as a real writer, not just someone who happens to write. I especially thank Linda Kay Silva and Liz Gibson for working around all my life changes during that year and making it possible for me to stay in class. I also appreciate Karelia Stetz-Waters, Julia Watts, Georgia Beers, Sandra Moran, and Carsen Taite for their instruction, encouragement, and homework feedback. Georgia Beers, my wonderful mentor for the last three months of that class, was especially helpful and I will be forever grateful for her guidance.

I sincerely thank Lee Fitzsimmons at Desert Palm Press for taking a chance on this first-time author, Mary Hettel, my editor, for helping me make this story what it is, and Michelle Brodeur for a great cover. I feel blessed to work with each of you.

Dedication

This book is dedicated to my partner and biggest cheerleader, Debbie Hilliard. You have believed in me since we met and have always been proud of what I do, making sure I have time and space to write even when our life gets hectic. Thanks for being excited about my writing obsession and putting up with all of this craziness. I hope I always make you proud.

Hurricane Season

CHAPTER ONE

CARRIE ALEXANDER PUSHED HER grocery cart through the Publix produce department, picking up one tomato and then another to regard the virtues of each one. As she looked over the latest selection, a woman scanning the lettuce in the bin along the wall caught her attention. Sunglasses perched in her short, wavy blonde hair, her tank top and Bermuda shorts showed off a lightly tanned, very fit body. Deciding she needed lettuce to go with those tomatoes, she threw the one in her hand into a plastic bag without really looking. She tried to move nonchalantly around the corner of the tomato bin, tripped over a crate of tangerines sitting on the floor, and fell straight into the woman in question. Strong arms grabbed her, holding her firmly.

"Oh my God, I'm so sorry," Carrie blurted, her face hot. She found herself looking straight into eyes the color of the Gulf of Mexico, and a face with a huge grin. "Uh, wow…how awkward. I'm so sorry," Carrie managed to stutter out as she regained her footing. Suddenly too embarrassed to do anything else, she extricated herself from the woman's grasp, muttered another "excuse me" as she retrieved her cart and quickly took off down the aisle. She headed to the self-checkout counter with what little she had in her basket, quickly paid for her purchases, and practically ran to her car.

She felt herself finally start to breathe normally once she plopped into the driver's seat. *Geez, what a disaster that was! I really made a fool of myself. Well, so much for that. More than likely I'm never going to see her again, so no big deal, right? Too bad…that woman was hot.* Carrie still felt her arm around her waist as if she had just been grabbed once more as she fell. More than anything else she was sure she'd never forget those amazing blue eyes.

***

Shawn Richards stood next to the lettuce bin staring after that pretty but perhaps slightly crazy woman with big brown eyes, who fell into her arms and then took off like she'd been shot. The woman didn't look back as she rushed away, so Shawn got a good chance to take in the cute butt and legs of the rescue-ee. Fort Myers female scenery had definitely improved in the several years since she'd lived here. Or maybe she was just noticing more now that she was single again. She couldn't help shaking her head and grinning as the look on that woman's face flashed once more through her mind. *Food, Shawn. You're here for food, not a woman. Yeah, but she certainly was nice to look at.*

It took Shawn nearly an hour to complete her shopping. There was nothing in the cupboards at the house except for what she had hauled in with her last night. She hadn't stayed at her Florida home for any length of time for several years, so the cupboards had been "Mother Hubbard" bare. With her shopping finished, Shawn loaded up the Jeep and headed back to the house.

Saying Southwest Florida is muggy even in early summer is akin to saying the sky is blue. It just is. Not an ideal time to acclimate herself to living there especially after having lived in San Francisco for several years. Damp was one thing, but this was past that and quite warm to go with it. It'd be the worst in August. As people around there were wont to say, though, that's what air conditioning was invented for.

She turned once more into her driveway, which was about six car lengths long and paved with crushed shells. Most of the neighbors had long ago repaved with asphalt or concrete, but she loved the crackling sound her tires made when she drove on the shells. It reminded her of her childhood. Her house, like most of the rest in the neighborhood, was in the old "cracker" style—elevated off the ground, wood siding, metal roof, and porches on the front and back, with the front one screened in. Although she remembered thinking the back porch could be expanded into a nice deck when she originally bought it, she'd never gotten around to it. She just hadn't been there long enough at a time until now to do anything to the place.

Hauling in the grocery bags, she noticed the air was heavy with the smell of incoming rain, typical for a Southwest Florida summer afternoon. That would be a relief, actually. She didn't have the energy to deal with the yard right then, so the push mower should give her a good workout tomorrow morning instead.

A short while later, juggling her Kindle and a glass of sweet tea,

Shawn took a sip of the cool liquid as she stepped out onto the front screened-in porch. She'd been looking forward to this first afternoon back home after a busy morning of shopping and unpacking. She settled into the cushions with an audible sigh after turning on the outside fan and pointing it toward her chair. Once settled, she propped her bare feet on the wooden porch rail, her toes against the coarse metal screen, and opened the latest installment of her favorite novel series.

Two chapters in, she looked up when she heard the palm fronds rustling louder than usual, and felt the first raindrops hitting her bare feet. She hated to abandon the porch; however, she had no choice this time. She flopped down on the sofa with one foot under her and leaned into the sofa arm pillow to resume reading just as the first thunder growled.

The room quickly darkened from the storm outside. Rain pinging on the metal roof of the porch beat a steady, almost hypnotic rhythm in between the rolls of thunder. Soothing and peaceful, it was just what she needed. She smiled as she reached for the switch on her favorite lamp. It had two intertwined fish on it in the sign of Pisces, her birth sign. In the pool of lamplight, she spotted a small picture in an oak frame that had escaped her notice since she arrived last night. She turned it around to look at it closer, and then wished she hadn't. There she was—Jen.

Someone had taken a picture of the two of them when they were on vacation in Colorado three years ago. They were laughing and holding long oars, like they were actually going to paddle down the rapids. Not that Jen would've done that, mind you. She never did anything that included getting wet or dirty. In spite of that, it'd been the best vacation they'd taken while they were together. She reached for the photo, took a deep breath as she gently stroked the image with her thumb before hurling it across the room, where it crashed landed upside down. She stared at the broken wooden frame and the shards of glass littering the floor. She'd clean that broken mess up later, just not right now.

Tears welled up, despite her effort to hold them back. She'd decided months ago not to let Jen do that to her any more, yet sometimes it happened anyway. Tasting salt as she licked her lips, she realized a single tear had escaped and rolled down her cheek to the corner of her mouth. She took another deep breath, wiped away the stray tear and its track, and headed to the kitchen to make herself a drink of something stronger than sweet tea.

CHAPTER TWO

CARRIE PULLED HER BIKE out for her usual morning ride, hoping to get it in before it was too hot for that kind of exercise. She walked her bike down the driveway and stopped at the street to adjust her helmet strap. As she looked to the right and left before taking off, she saw a woman in a baseball cap, running shorts, and tank, running at a fairly fast clip down the road.

First, seeing someone she didn't know running on her street was very unusual. Second, wow – two women who made her look twice in two days, also quite unusual. Granted, there was no way to know if she was really that great looking from behind, but with a body like that it would be a sin if she wasn't. She actually looked a lot like the woman from yesterday at Publix. Built sleek like a racecar, she ran with no wasted motion—so smoothly her head barely bobbed up and down. She watched for a few more seconds, enjoying the view until the woman turned into a driveway down the street and was nearly out of sight. She shook her head and smiled, got on her bike and took off for her ride.

***

Shawn turned into her driveway at the end of her morning run, and stopped to walk the rest of the way. Just as she stopped, movement at the edge of her field of vision caught her attention and curiosity made her look down the street. She saw a woman riding her bike away from her—a woman that looked sort of like the same one she caught in the store yesterday. She chuckled to herself as she replayed the incident again in her head. Nah, can't be. What are the chances? Besides, she couldn't tell much from looking at just her behind and with the helmet on. Still there was a definite resemblance. Just then, a little voice in her head started in as she walked into the house. *What are you thinking? Don't even contemplate another woman right now. Don't even start.*

Move along Shawn.

This morning she decided to get back to work on the article she was writing for Sunbelt Life and try to get more work done on her novel. She still needed to get back out to Sanibel Island for an up-to-date feel for the article. While she was reworking the outline, her e-mail dinged at her. It was a note from one of her favorite people on the planet, her cousin Greg. She had told him she was coming back to Florida and he was checking to be sure she made it. An invitation to lunch was also included, suggesting they meet at Fort Myers Beach when she had the time. She reached for her phone and tapped in his number.

"Hey cuz," she said when he answered. "I'm here."

"So when did you get in? Ready for a trip to the beach yet?" Greg said in his usual cheerful voice.

"I just got in yesterday. I'm not quite ready for anything except for some work and sleep, though. Several days of driving will do that. How about tomorrow for lunch? I loved The Beached Whale the last time we went there. Is it still open?"

"Yep, still open and still very busy. During the week at lunch shouldn't be too bad. I'm dying to hear all about everything, but I'll wait until I see you. Have a client in ten minutes. How about twelve thirty, or would earlier work better for you?"

"Twelve thirty is fine. Looking forward to it. Love you, cuz."

"Love you, too. See you tomorrow."

Nice. I have something to look forward to. At least there would be something besides more work, heat and the humidity. And probably more rain. Bit of a change from the San Francisco Bay Area, heat-wise, anyway. For now, it's back to work.

She stared at the laptop screen, waiting for something to come to her worth hitting the keys to type in. She decided to just keep typing anything that came to mind and hoped that something could be edited out of it that was good enough to use. *Don't think about anything else. Just keep working. Keep going.* For some reason, her brain wasn't cooperating fully.

That stupid picture of Jen. She couldn't remember even bringing it here, let alone leaving it behind. Must've been that short visit the last time, a couple of years ago. She couldn't believe she thought it was important enough to bring down here. Of course, she hadn't thought it would all be over so quickly. That was the one that was supposed to be forever. It wasn't. Not even close.

Shawn stopped staring at the laptop and stretched out her long legs. She still needed to edit that last bit, but it could wait till after lunch. As she barefooted across the wood floor to the kitchen, she was startled when her phone broke the silence.

Caller ID said it was Alexis Jackson, her publisher. *Uh, oh.* "Hey AJ," she greeted her old friend, trying to sound casual.

"Hey yourself. Are you on vacation down there or actually working on that book?"

"I'm working on it," she said. "In fact I'm just now taking a lunch break. Even writers have to eat sometimes."

"Yeah, well, you know it's due in less than thirty days. I even gave you extra time because of that situation you had. Since this one is the last of this series, your fans are chomping at the bit to get at it. *Witching Hour* should be one of your best sellers at this rate," AJ said. "Providing of course that you're writing it. You are, right?"

"Yeah, I'm working on it. You know I'll get it finished. It's nearly done, and then you can have it to tear apart."

"Very funny. Now listen, I'm sorry about what happened, and I'm not trying to be mean about it. You know it's been quite a while now and you need to move on. We can probably let you have a little more time if you need it, but promise me you'll do your best. No meltdowns at the last minute."

"I promise. Now how about I get some food into your favorite author so she can get back to the word mine." Shawn opened the door to the refrigerator. "Hey, if you get bored up there, come on down for a long weekend. We can hang out at the beach or maybe even take the shuttle boat down to Key West for a couple of days and play Hemingway."

"Oh, no, you don't. You're not using me as an excuse to play hooky. I'd love to get together after you present me with your latest rendering, though. We can have a great time then, and not before…unless you're having issues… You aren't, are you?"

"Nah, I'm fine. Just tired after all that driving. Hey, let me get back to some sustenance, please? Talk to you soon."

Shawn hit "end" on the phone before she could press her any further. She didn't need to 'talk' about it. AJ knew this, but she was trying to be a friend, and Shawn couldn't fault her for that.

CHAPTER THREE

SHAWN SMILED AS SHE turned from Summerlin onto San Carlos Boulevard toward Fort Myers Beach. She passed the familiar colorful seaside stores that had been there for decades selling swimsuits, shorts, towels, and T-shirts. Even from a little over a mile away, the salty smell of the Gulf wafted in the Jeep's open window. Mixed in with the T-shirt shops, fishing outfitters and boat marinas, brightly painted seafood restaurants with signs that looked like huge tropical fish lured in the passer-by.

Crossing the bridge onto the island always felt good to her, and especially today she couldn't help grinning as she drove. She'd been looking forward to having lunch with Greg all morning. After making a left onto Estero Boulevard, she had to stop several times to avoid the people wandering across the street at odd places. Tourists were the lifeblood of Fort Myers Beach. Although they could sometimes be a pain when they ignored the traffic around them, she certainly didn't want to hit one of them. She was looking forward to a nice long lunch with some great seafood and one of her favorite people.

The Beached Whale was on the left and Greg was standing on the veranda—tall, lean, suntanned, and grinning from ear to ear when he saw her. He waved and came to meet her as she parked. He was one of the few in the family who accepted who she was at face value and loved her for herself. Ten years older than her own thirty-eight years, her cousin had been her hero as a child. Now, they were more like close friends.

"So good to see you!" Greg hugged her tight the minute she got out of her Wrangler, and then held her out at arm's length as he looked her up and down. "You look great and I love the new shorter hair. It fits you."

Shawn ran her fingers through her short sandy locks. "Thanks. I needed a change. And you don't look so bad yourself. You never seem to get any older. How come I get older but you never do?"

"It's a secret," he whispered, followed by a laugh. "Good genes, I guess. You know my dad has never stopped looking like a handsome forty year old. Are you starving? I sure am."

Greg and Shawn stepped onto the wooden deck that surrounded *The Beached Whale* on three sides and into the cool shade of the restaurant. The hostess nodded at them and pointed to the back stairs. Up a set of well-worn wooden treads they found the upper deck and a nice breeze. They chose a table with wooden benches, right by the deck railing and under a turquoise umbrella for shade. A waiter clad in a bright blue tropical shirt took their orders of sweet tea and grouper sandwiches before he quickly disappeared.

Shawn took a deep breath, leaned back, and spread her arms across the back of the sun-bleached wooden bench. Her gaze wandered across the two lane street below, following the path to the wide strip of bright white sugary sand leading to the turquoise water of the Gulf of Mexico. For a moment she was again a six year old, playing on that same stretch of beach and running in the surf as her mother watched. She sighed and breathed in the familiar aromas of salt, wet seaweed, and fish. Brightly clad tourists walking by beneath them on the boardwalk contributed the scents of various coconut-concoctions of suntan oil which drifted up on the Gulf breeze.

"So, what're you up to these days?" Greg asked, breaking Shawn's reverie. "Seems like quite a while since we talked. Still writing those bodice rippers?"

"Oh, you're so funny. You know very well I don't write that heaving bosom stuff. I do have another book almost finished, but for some reason I'm just not satisfied with it. I have a magazine article going as well, and can't seem to finish that, either. I'm headed over to Sanibel after lunch for a little updated color for that article. Want to come?"

"I'd love to, but I've got an appointment with a client this afternoon about two thirty. I think you'll be surprised at how nice it's looking out there, though. The last time you were on Sanibel was probably not long after the cleanup after Charley, wasn't it?"

Shawn nodded. "Yeah, it's been a long time. By the way, I need to ask for your input on something. I'm thinking about adding a room onto my place. Since I'm going to live here full time now, I definitely need more space."

The waiter returned with two large glasses of sweet tea, and disappeared again.

Greg took a sip of his tea. "Yeah, your place is pretty small. It was fine for one person who wasn't there much, which you weren't. Or for spending a short vacation with one other person."

"I know. I don't want to buy another house since I love the one I have." Shawn reached for her spoon, dipped out a piece of crushed ice and chewed it slowly. "It's just feeling cramped. I think the only option is to expand, since my lot is plenty big enough. I like the style of it, so I'd like to find someone who'd stay true to that old cracker house. The tin roof, raised porch, and center hallway layout works well for me, although I'd love to set up a real office instead of writing on my laptop literally on my lap on the sofa or at the kitchen table. I also have a lot of books that need a home."

Greg smiled. "I get it. I'm very happy to hear you're making it a home now. That means you're staying for sure?"

Shawn grinned back. "Yeah, that's the plan. Can you recommend anyone?"

"I can. Gladstone Construction," he said without hesitation. "They're even on your side of the river and they do great work."

"How do you know them? Have you used them?"

"No, I haven't actually used them myself. They're my clients. I upgraded their computer system earlier this year," he said. "Check out their website, too. They do additions as well as ground up stuff. I got to know Rich Gladstone quite well while working on his system. He's a good guy and the company has a great reputation. You're welcome to tell him I recommended him and that you're my cousin. Even without that, I know he'd give you a fair price and come in on time. That's just the way he does business." Greg pulled out his phone and looked up some information on it, took out one of his own business cards and wrote on the back. "I'm putting Rich's office info on here and if you want, I'll call him and tell him you'll be calling."

"That works, thanks." She took the card and shoved it into her shorts pocket. "I'm looking forward to getting this stage of settling in over with."

Greg took a sip of his sweet tea. "I notice you're here by yourself. That really means you and Jen are over with?"

"Yeah, it's definitely done." Shawn pushed her already sweating glass of sweet tea around in its puddle. "I'm glad, to tell you the truth. It was over long before it was over, if you know what I mean. She's been gone nearly a year, now. I guess it took me this long to realize I needed to come home."

"I do know what you mean. It's not easy, but one day you wake up and realize it's time to get on with your life. I'm so glad you came home. Maybe you'll meet some nice, sweet local girl and fall in love again."

"Oh, God, not for a long time!" Shawn waved her hands in front of her face, warding off even the idea. "I'm not going to go through that again anytime soon."

CHAPTER FOUR

CARRIE WAS JUST BACK from a late lunch when the phone rang. She was greeted with the familiar bass voice of her boss, Rich Gladstone. "You remember Greg, the guy who redid our computer system?"

"Of course I do. He spent a lot of time with me while he was figuring out what we needed."

"Well, he's sending some business our way. His cousin just moved back here, and she's interested in having us add an office onto her house. Her name is Shawn Richards. I told her to come in tomorrow morning at ten, since I knew Simon cancelled. I know I should've called you first to check. Tell me you didn't schedule anyone else in there yet."

Carrie pulled up the appointment calendar. "No, I didn't. You do have a meeting with Brad at nine, but that'll give you a good reason to keep him from going on longer than an hour. Ms. Richards is now on your calendar for ten." She grinned. "You didn't do anything else I need to know about, did you?" She could hear him laughing.

"Right, I know. Not this time, though. See you in an hour."

Carrie always gave Rich a hard time, part of their easy working relationship. Rich told her fairly often how smart he'd been to hire her. Even if he hadn't known her father, he said she was far and away the best assistant he had ever had except for maybe his wife. And when his wife wasn't listening, he told her she was in a class by herself. His wife had not worked in the office for a long time, since raising a house full of boys took most of her time. He always told his wife that every assistant had to measure up to her. Carrie thought that was sweet. She wished she had someone to love her like that.

Carrie took a deep breath and let out a sigh as she fiddled with some papers on her desk. She just wasn't herself today. Her mind was still on those gorgeous blue eyes she saw at Publix. Not to mention those strong arms that held her for an instant. *Geez, girl. Get over it and get back to work. That woman is probably not your kind and you're barking up the wrong tree.* A few hours later Carrie was on her way home. She thought maybe she should stop by Publix again, just in the off chance that same woman would be there, but she reconsidered, thinking that would be just downright silly.

As she approached her driveway, she caught a glimpse of someone running down the road. Looking closer, she realized she looked like the woman she saw running a couple of days ago. For a minute, she wondered again who she was. Since that was twice in such a short time, she must either live nearby or be visiting someone in the area. It was time to get changed and out on the bike for a few miles and just what she needed to get her mind off those blue eyes for a while.

A bit later, dressed in bike shorts and a tank, dark curls pulled back in a ponytail, she walked her bike to the end of the driveway. As she paused to put her helmet on, she saw the same woman running toward her. The woman slowed down and stopped when she saw her.

"Hey!" the woman said without removing her sunglasses. "You live here?"

"Yeah, I do," Carrie said. "I saw you on your way out earlier. Do you live around here?"

"Just down the street," she said, pulling up the front of her tank top to wipe the sweat off her face.

Carrie noticed the woman looking her over slowly. *Oh brother, another of God's gifts to the world of women.* "I'm Carrie," she said, holding out her hand.

The woman wiped her right hand on her shorts and then briefly shook Carrie's hand. "Shawn. Nice to meet you." She grinned. "I'll see you around then." She took off running, waving without looking back.

Carrie chuckled. No doubt about it, that woman had an amazing body, but she wasn't much on conversation. Oh well, at least she said hi. She sure looked a lot like the woman she ran into in Publix, but she couldn't be sure. She'd only seen her for a few seconds and mostly what she remembered about her were her eyes. Without her sunglasses, she would've known for sure. Carrie shook her head, and started pedaling down the road in the direction Shawn had been running from.

***

Smooth move, Shawn. Really, could you have been snottier? She stopped at her driveway and glanced down the road. *Yep, she's the woman I saw the other day on the bike and she looked like the same woman from Publix. She's undeniably cute. One thing's for sure, the neighborhood has definitely improved. Maybe I should be neighborly and invite her over some time. Not tonight, though. I've got work to do and an appointment in the morning at the construction company office.*

CHAPTER FIVE

SHAWN WALKED INTO GLADSTONE Construction ten minutes before her appointment time. Based on her cousin's description of the company, she was surprised to see that it had a rather small office. A nicely appointed waiting room greeted her, with just a few chairs and….*the woman from yesterday afternoon? What was her name, Carly? No, Carrie. At least she looks a lot like her.*

The receptionist and object of her scrutiny was on the phone with someone. She glanced up, smiled and waved to let her know that she'd be right with her. Shawn sat in one of the available chairs and waited for her to be free. Meantime, she managed to take a closer look at Carrie without staring at her. *Dark curly hair, big brown eyes, yep, that was the woman from yesterday.*

Shawn walked up to the desk when the receptionist was free. "Shawn Richards to see Rich Gladstone at ten."

Carrie smiled what looked like her receptionist smile at Shawn. "Good morning, Ms. Richards. He's expecting you. Nice to see you again. He should be out in just a minute or two. You're welcome to have a seat and wait."

Shawn grinned and leaned on the counter in front of Carrie's desk. "Nice to see you again, too."

"So, I understand you're planning to have some work done on your house. Adding on an office?"

"Yes, I need more space…nothing big," she said, still leaning on the counter.

Just then, a man stepped out of the office door to the right, followed by another man, who kept talking. Carrie excused herself, went over to them, and said a few words Shawn couldn't hear to the first man, who turned to look at her. He smiled as he strode across the carpeted waiting area and reached out his hand. "Hi, I'm Rich. You must be Shawn."

Shawn nodded and shook his hand. "I am. Thanks for seeing me so quickly."

"Come on back. I had a client call yesterday morning to cancel his appointment today, so it worked out great. Greg told me a lot about you. Seems he's rather proud of his author cousin. It's nice to meet you."

"He told me quite a bit about you, too. He thinks quite highly of you and your company."

"The feeling is definitely mutual," he said as they walked toward Rich's office. "Now let's see what we can do for you."

Shawn followed Rich into his office, which was just big enough for a sofa, chair, and his desk without appearing overcrowded, along with a table holding blueprints in the corner by the window. A big twelve-paned window behind his desk looked out over the corporate yard. Lots of bookshelves lined two of the walls. There were many shelves holding books, small trophies and awards. The scent of paper and leather also greeted her. Looking around, she tried to imagine what she wanted in her office, but she kept seeing Carrie. She shook her head to clear the image. *What kind of nonsense was that?*

Rich offered Shawn some coffee or water and motioned for her to have a seat on the sofa. Shawn accepted a bottle of cold water and sat, immediately deciding she liked the idea of a leather sofa. Over the next half hour, Shawn and Rich discussed what she was looking for in more detail. Returning to the lobby, Rich had Carrie check his schedule for open field appointments.

"How about two on Friday afternoon? Does that work for both of you?" Carrie asked. Shawn agreed, and gave Carrie a business card with her home address and phone number handwritten on the back. She shook Rich's hand and smiled at Carrie, and was out the door seconds later.

***

"Rich, she lives down the street from me," Carrie said.

"Really? How nice. Do you know her?"

"Actually, I ran into her at Publix a few days ago. And by 'ran into her,' I mean actually ran into her next to the lettuce bin. I tripped over a box of something and fell right into her. It was so embarrassing, I hope she doesn't remember that part. Then last night we met at the end of my driveway. She was on her way back from her run and I was on my way out for a bike ride. The second time I saw her she was wearing a baseball cap and sunglasses. I wasn't sure she was the same woman until she came in today…She seems nice enough."

"Nice enough? Hmm…I think she might be someone you'd like to get to know, since you read so much. She's a writer."

"Really? Okay, now that's interesting." Carrie watched out the front window as Shawn walked out to her Jeep.

"Greg told me a little bit about her. While she was in my office, I asked her for more about what she does, since we're going to design and build an office onto her house. So her name doesn't sound familiar at all?"

"Nope, I don't think so, although I'll definitely look her up later. Maybe I've read something she's written and just don't recognize her name." Carrie mulled this information for a few seconds. "Did she say whether she writes books or for a magazine?"

"You know what, she did say she wrote books."

"By any chance did she give you the name of any of them?"

"Hmm, I think she said her last one was *Grand Compulsion* or something like that. I didn't recognize it, but then again I'm not much of a fiction reader, myself, and with a name like that, I'd assume it's fiction."

"I'll check her out on the Internet. If she's written anything much at all, it'll be searchable."

"You do that. I'm curious myself, now, so let me know what you find out." He turned to head back to his office.

"Don't forget you have that conference call in ten minutes," she called out.

"On it. Thanks."

As Rich retreated to his office, Carrie tried to think if she'd ever read anything by an author named Richards, but couldn't think of one. A search on Amazon for a book called Grand Compulsion yielded nothing. Of course, Rich could've been wrong about the title. She didn't see any books by a Shawn Richards either. The closest she could come to Shawn Richards was her favorite author, S.K. Richardson. Oh well, maybe later she'd find her on another website or under some obscure literary publisher. Who knows, she might even write textbooks or the like.

Carrie was sure she needed to find out more about this Shawn person, and those blue eyes had to have something to do with it. Okay, living down the street from a real, honest-to-God author had something else to do with it. *But those eyes…*She sighed and leaned back in her chair for a moment. Those blue eyes were stunning. She knew she could drown in their depths. That could be dangerous.

***

Shawn stepped out of the Gladstone office, slipped on her aviator sunglasses, slapped on an Atlanta Braves baseball cap, and slid into her Jeep. She sat there for a few seconds, smiled, and shook her head. *Yep, that Carrie was cute for sure; however, it's not a good idea to flirt with a neighbor. In fact, it's usually a very bad idea, but she sure is cute*, a little voice in her head said. She chuckled to herself, and started the Jeep to head home.

Just before suppertime, Shawn sauntered down her driveway and started her run by walking down the street before starting to jog. She had just started to speed up to a run when she saw Carrie at the end of her driveway.

"Oh, hi," she called out, and then smiled. "It's you again." She stopped at Carrie's driveway.

"Hi yourself," Carrie called back, buckling her bike helmet. She pushed her bike onto the street. "Looks like we're neighbors."

"Just over there, second house down on the left." Shawn pointed down the street.

"I didn't know anyone lived there." Carrie pulled on some riding gloves. "In fact, I don't think I've seen anyone around there since I moved in here two years ago."

"I just got back. I've been living in California for a while."

"Really...well, welcome back then. Are you on vacation or do you live here now?" Carrie asked, and apparently thought better of it. "You know what, that's really none of my business..."

"Oh, that's okay. As a matter of fact, I'm pretty sure I'm back to stay. I grew up around here. Anyway, nice to see you again. Sorry if I delayed your ride. Catch you later." Shawn resumed her run, waving again without looking to see if Carrie was watching. A couple of minutes later, she looked back just as Carrie and her bike turned off on a side road.

An hour later, Shawn stopped running at the end of her driveway and paused before glancing back up the street toward Carrie's house. She wasn't sure what she was looking for, but all she saw was a neighbor's Sheltie trotting down the road, stopping here and there to sniff something among the queen palms lining the street. She shrugged, turned and headed to the house. Back to work. AJ was going to shoot her if this book wasn't finished soon—friend or no friend. .

CHAPTER SIX

AROUND ELEVEN FRIDAY MORNING Shawn sat hunched over her laptop, iced tea glass in one hand, when the phone rang. Without looking, she reached for it and hit the answer button.

"Shawn," she answered, checking the Caller ID at the same time. It was Gladstone Construction.

"Hi, Shawn. Carrie from Gladstone. I hope I'm not interrupting your work."

"No problem at all. What can I do for you?"

"I'm confirming your appointment with Rich. Is two this afternoon still good?"

Shawn glanced down at her watch. "Yeah, sure. I'll want a break by then anyway. Two it still is. Are you coming with him?"

"Uh, no...I don't usually do that. He makes his own notes. Why'd you ask?"

"I don't know. I just wondered, that's all." Shawn stalled. "I haven't seen you for a few days and thought maybe I'd see you today."

Carrie laughed. Shawn immediately decided she liked the sound of that. "Aww...you missed me. No one else to bother down the street?"

"No, actually there hasn't been, as a matter of fact. So my runs have been rather boring."

"I've been busy myself the last few days and haven't had time for a ride. I have to admit I've missed it."

"Not me, though? I'm crushed." Shawn chuckled. "Maybe I'll see you later on."

"Um...anyway...Rich will be there at two then. Bye." And Carrie was gone.

Shawn stared at the phone for a few seconds after Carrie hung up. She ran her fingers through her hair. *Stop flirting with her. Get back to work.*

***

Shawn next looked up when she heard the sound of a pickup turning into her driveway. *Was it already two o'clock?* She got to the door just in time to see the Gladstone logo on the side and greet Rich as he got out of his truck.

"Hey, come on in," she called to him and waved. "I've got some iced tea for after the grand tour. How does that sound?"

Rich reached out to shake her hand. "Hi. That would be great. Thanks. So, where were you thinking about putting your office?"

For the next few minutes, she gave him the tour, which didn't take very long. The front door opened into an open hallway that ran from the front door to the back. Off to the right was the small living room with the brick fireplace, and behind that the kitchen and dining nook. The one and only bedroom was off the left of the hall directly across from the living room, with the bathroom and utility room located off the kitchen in the back of the house. The back door opened onto a small porch just big enough for a couple of chairs and a little table. The entire house was decorated in beach style, with white wicker furniture and light colors. The exception was the living room sofa, which was a rich marine blue with white throw pillows.

After they reviewed what she wanted in her office, and where she would like to have it, they walked around the outside of the house deciding where the new office should be. As it turned out, the best spot for the new office was going to be where her bedroom currently was. Rich suggested the addition of a new master bedroom and bath on the other side of the house. He also gave her a few ideas about other things that could be upgraded without breaking the budget, while still keeping the feel of the older home. That decided, he promised to get back to her with some drawings and prices.

Rich backed out of the driveway as Shawn felt a big smile form on her face, thinking about really living in her old home. She could see why Greg thought so highly of Rich Gladstone, he obviously cared about his work. She knew it was time to make this house a real home, not just a landing pad before she took off again on another adventure somewhere. *Home. What a pleasant thought.* Plus, she might see more of Carrie if she came to Rich's office again, even if she didn't see her much on the street. She found herself looking forward to seeing Carrie this afternoon at the end of her driveway.

Hold it, she argued with herself. *This is already getting out of hand here. She's the woman down the street—just a nice neighbor. She probably has a boyfriend or girlfriend who could beat the crap out of me anyway. Good grief. I really, really, do not need to chase another woman right now, no matter how cute she is. A friend, I could use, though, and it's always a good idea to be neighborly.*

BJ Phillips

CHAPTER SEVEN

BEFORE CARRIE PULLED INTO her own driveway, she watched as she passed the house she was sure was Shawn's. The brick red Jeep in the driveway probably meant Shawn was home. She smiled when she thought about possibly finding her at the end of the driveway again this afternoon.

She piddled around in the house for a bit after changing her riding shorts three times to find a pair that she thought looked the best on her, the royal blue ones with a grey stripe down the outside of each leg. After turning around several times in front of the mirror to be sure this was the outfit she wanted, she put her house key in her wrist pocket and headed for her bike. Sure enough, just as she got to the end of her driveway, there was Shawn.

"I was just wondering if you'd you like to drop by after your ride for something cold to drink," Shawn said. "Iced tea, or maybe a margarita? I make great margaritas and my iced tea isn't bad, either. We can sit on the porch. Neighborly like, you know?" Shawn added that last part in her best southern drawl.

"Well, that would be very neighborly. And I do like margaritas...How about after my ride I come home and take a quick shower first. I can stop by on my way back to give you a heads up, then you can give me a few minutes to get cleaned up. How does that sound?"

"Sounds good to me. See you in a bit." Shawn whistled as she began jogging, and then broke into a run with a grin on her face. A few minutes later, she decided to cut her run short so she could get back and clean up before Carrie returned.

Half an hour later, Shawn was headed to the kitchen humming to herself as she dragged out the blender and the margarita ingredients. Ten minutes after that, she had everything ready, including some lime slices for the glasses.

She grinned to herself, picturing Carrie sitting on her porch with a margarita in her hand. She decided to wait outside. No, that would look a bit too eager. She decided to wait in the house. *No, I wouldn't see Carrie coming up the drive. I'll wait on the porch after all, acting like I just got out there. Silly. Sit on the porch with my Kindle, reading. Yes, that would strike the right pose. Put my feet up on the porch rail. Yeah, that looks nonchalant enough.* In no time, she was so engrossed in the latest book from her favorite author that she didn't see someone coming up the drive on her bike.

"Hey Shawn!" Carrie called out from the driveway. Shawn startled and nearly fell over backward in her chair. That set Carrie laughing so hard, she nearly had to sit down herself.

"Wow that must be a great book!" Carrie wiped her eyes on her shirt. "I'll be back in about twenty minutes, is that okay? And I'm definitely looking forward to one of those famous margaritas of yours." She turned her bike around and headed back down the driveway, still laughing.

Mortified, Shawn recovered her Kindle from the floor and mentally picked herself up as well. She'll be back in just a few minutes, she reminded herself. A short time later, Shawn heard Carrie's sandals crunching on the driveway.

"You didn't have to bring anything," Shawn said, eyeing the bag in Carrie's hand.

"No, I didn't, however I thought we could use something to eat since it's almost dinner time. I don't know about you, but I'm hungry." Carrie held up the bag. "It's nothing special, just some French bread, salami, some grapes, and cheese. I already cut them up, so we just have to put them on something. Any plate will do. We can eat these and sip on your margaritas."

"A woman after my own heart, for sure. I'm always hungry," Shawn reached for the bag and headed for the kitchen. "Have a seat and I'll be right back."

A few minutes later, margarita in one hand, and some bread, salami, and cheese in the other, Shawn propped her bare feet back up on the porch rail and sighed happily. "Now this is a nice evening. You know, I could do this often."

Carrie sighed as well and leaned back in her chair. "Yes, this is very pleasant." She popped a grape into her mouth.

"Seriously, it's great to have someone to sit here with. Thanks for bringing over this excellent fare." Shawn reached for another bite-sized piece of French bread and a piece of cheese.

"Excellent margaritas, too." Carrie held her glass up in a salute then took another sip. "If you don't mind my asking, what were you doing in California? Rich told me you're an author, but I assume you can write anywhere." She plopped one bare foot then another on the porch rail next to Shawn's.

Shawn looked away from Carrie's pale pink polished toes, which were only inches from her own and considered the paint on the porch ceiling. Didn't help. Carrie's toes were too interesting. She looked back, meanwhile pretending she was looking out into the yard. "Well, that's true to a point. I was writing a series of books all set in the San Francisco Bay Area, and it helped to be there. Then after a while there was another reason."

"Ah, from the sound of it, I'll bet it was a 'somebody' reason."

"Right you are," Shawn took another sip of her drink. She glanced over at Carrie to see her reaction. "A woman." No reaction. "Anyway, it was time to come home."

"Home...meaning here?"

"I'm a Floridian born and bred, so yes, this is home. It was fun for a while in California, but that's over. I had to come back here to, and please forgive the expression, 'find' myself." She held her fingers in the air like little quotation marks. "What about you? What brings you to living here? Did you grow up here?"

Carrie took a sip of her margarita and gazed into her glass. "Pretty much. Well, I wasn't doing anything romantic like writing. I've lived in this area for most of my life, and my grandmother lived in the house I live in now."

As Carrie paused, Shawn noticed a little faraway smile on Carrie's face and assumed she was remembering her grandmother.

"So do you like working for a construction company?"

"I love what I do. I love the people I work with and I make enough to be happy. So here I am. I have some friends in the area but I mostly spend my time at work or riding my bike. I read a lot, too."

"Just never know where you'll end up, do you." Shawn noted that Carrie hadn't mentioned a boyfriend or girlfriend. Interesting. "What do you like to read?"

"Oh, all kinds of stuff, whatever jumps off the shelf and begs me to read it. Everything from mysteries to biographies. I'll admit to a weakness for romances, though. If you're ever looking for something to read, I've probably got something you'd like."

"Sounds like you're quite the book lover. I might take you up on that, since I love to read, too. Well, I'm happy to have you for a neighbor." Shawn held her glass up for a toast. "Here's to good neighbors!"

Carrie clinked her glass with Shawn's. "Most definitely. Good neighbors," she said. Their eyes lingered on each other for just a few seconds longer than necessary as they laughed.

CHAPTER EIGHT

SHAWN ENDED UP MOVING her bed to the living room while her bedroom was being remodeled into an office, and her new bedroom and bath additions were under construction. She had to put most of her living room items in storage for the duration. While it was fun seeing her new office take shape, it was not fun sleeping in the living room until she realized she could lie in bed and watch television, which eased the pain.

The second day of construction, Carrie stopped by on her way home to see what was taking shape, finding Shawn on the front porch. "It looks pretty hard to live in, but I bet it's exciting to watch the construction, isn't it?"

"Most of the time. Right this minute, though, I think I could use an easy path from the front of the house to the kitchen and bathroom. Rich said it won't be much longer until I have that back. Right now, though, it's still sort of difficult. I just have to zigzag my way through stuff. The construction crew is mostly going in and out of the back door while they remodel my old bedroom into the new office because it's easier. Oh well, at least I can still sit on the front porch."

"Aww, poor baby. How about we take your mind off all this and you can join me for supper down at the Smokin' Pit? I assume you like barbeque, right?"

"Are you kidding? Of course I like barbeque. I used to love that place. I don't know why, but for some reason haven't been there since I got back. They probably still have the best pulled pork in town, huh? Not to mention their baked beans."

"Yep, they still do. Give me about fifteen minutes, if that's enough for you. I just need to run home and take care of a couple of things."

"No problem. How about I pick you up?"

"Works for me, but remember this is my treat."

Shawn watched as Carrie pulled out of her driveway. Grinning, she fist-pumped a "yes!" and headed to her makeshift closet for a change of clothes. Fifteen minutes later dressed in a pair of navy cargo shorts and a pale blue polo shirt, she stuffed her wallet into her pocket, grabbed the keys and was out the door.

Carrie was waiting for her in front of her house. As she got into the Jeep, Shawn noticed a slight hint of cleavage at the top of Carrie's blouse. That was just enough to make one wonder what the rest looked like and could be a definite distraction this evening. Shawn mentally shook herself and decided she'd better keep her eyes on the road.

The Smokin' Pit was always busy, even on a weeknight, and this was no exception. Within a block of the place, the luscious smells of barbecued pork and beef as well as baked beans wafted out and grabbed passersby. Inside the rustic, timber-sided restaurant, the wooden tables had various pieces of local memorabilia embedded into the thick layers of acrylic covering the tops. Bouncy country music was just loud enough to enjoy without drowning out conversations. Shawn and Carrie didn't have to wait very long for a booth for two.

Carrie and Shawn were barely seated when a woman slid into the booth next to Carrie and put her arm around her for a hug. "Hey, gorgeous! What've you been up to? I haven't seen you for a while," she said. "And I see you brought a friend. How 'bout you introduce us?"

Carrie hugged the woman back. "Shawn, this is my friend Jess. We've known each other since grade school and she works here. Jess, this is my neighbor, Shawn. Gladstone is doing some work on her house."

Shawn felt herself being scrutinized intently as she stuck her hand out and Jess grasped it firmly. "Nice to meet you," they said at the same time.

Shawn was already sure she didn't like the way Jess was sitting there a little too close to Carrie. She wondered if there had been more to their relationship at one time besides just friends. It sure looked like there had been, the way Jess was draped all over her.

"We don't want to keep you away from your many customers here tonight," Shawn said, using her best genuine, but not genuine, smile.

"It's busy like this most of the time. I've always got time for Carrie here, though." Jess gave Carrie's shoulder another squeeze. "Listen, hon," she said directly to Carrie, "How about we get together this weekend for a little fun on the water? We can take the boat out."

"Oh, I don't know, Jess. Although that does sound like fun, I do have some tentative plans. How about I let you know on Friday?"

Shawn saw Jess glance briefly at her, followed by a smile back at Carrie. "Of course you can. I don't have any other plans for this weekend yet, and you know how I love cruising the river." She turned to Shawn. "Nice meeting you. Hope you enjoy your dinner. Guess we'll see you around then."

Jess gave Carrie another little sideways hug and left.

Carrie grinned. "Isn't she something? She's quite a character. She neglected to mention that she runs this place for the owners."

"Yes, and I'll bet she's good at it, too. I did notice you two seem quite close."

"Well, we did date for a while, over a year ago."

"She seems to still like you quite a bit. She was pretty cuddly over there." *And the question of which team Carrie bats for had been answered.*

"Oh, that's just Jess being Jess. I don't pay her any mind when she does things like that. She's kind of a touchy-feely person. She's quite the flirt and always has been."

Shawn wasn't so sure about Jess just being Jess. She had seen the sly look in her direction and the possessive way Jess kept her arm around Carrie. She didn't think she liked the looks of Jess draped over her. The waiter arrived with glasses full of ice and a pitcher of tea, quickly took their orders for pulled pork sandwiches and ribs, and disappeared again.

While they waited for their food to arrive, they looked at all the interesting things embedded in their tabletop. Pictures, matchbooks, a fifties brochure from The Alligator Farm and lots more were suspended in the acrylic. They laughed at the various items they pointed out to each other. Carrie pointed to a photograph in front of Shawn showing a man holding up some fish in one hand and holding a little dark haired girl with pigtails in the crook of his other arm. "That's my grandfather and that little girl is my Aunt Carrie."

Shawn looked closer at the picture. There was a resemblance. "So you were named after her, I'm guessing?"

"Yes, I was. When I was little my parents told me I looked a lot like her. She died before I was born, though, so I never knew her. I don't know how that picture wound up here in the table, but I'm happy it is. I get to see her as a little girl every time I sit here. There are lots of pictures of local people here on these tables." Carrie swept her hand across the table. Since your family is from around here, there could be someone you're related to or know on one them, too, if they were here back in the forties and fifties. You'd have to sit at every single one of these tables to find out. That's part of the fun of this place."

"Guess I'll have to just keep coming back till I have checked out all the tables," Shawn sipped on her tea. "You know, as many times as I used to come here, I never thought these were local pictures, so I never paid any attention to them. My parents never said anything about them. I figured they were just some pictures from somewhere, anywhere, that filled in the space. Heck, they could have come from unidentified boxes of yard-sale pictures."

They both laughed. Carrie's pulled pork sandwich and Shawn's ribs arrived, accompanied by heaps of French fries on each plate and a bowl each of those famous baked beans. The aromas of tangy sweet barbeque sauce and baked beans were mouth-watering. The rolls of paper towels on the end of each table attested to the wonderfully expected messiness coming with each meal.

"This stuff is pure heaven." Shawn licked her fingers in between bites of the ribs.

"It sure is," Carrie said, wiping her own mouth. "So when you came here as a kid, what was your favorite dish?"

"It's always been the ribs. I'd sometimes get the chicken, but the ribs...to die for. Even then I could put away the whole order of ribs, along with everything that came with it. And I didn't get the child's plate version either, once I got to about eight."

"Really? That's a lot of food for a kid. And you're telling me you ate the whole thing?"

"Yup. I was non-stop, high energy growing up. I needed that fuel to keep going. What about you, what was your favorite?"

"I used to go for the chicken legs. Guess they appeal to a lot of kids here, because I've seen them on quite a few tables." She paused, then laughed. "Mom said I liked them because the legs had 'handles' on them."

Shawn laughed, too, envisioning a little Carrie with her chicken with handles. "I love it. You must have been a cute kid. At least you had fun ideas. I'm rather surprised we never knew each other growing up. This isn't a very large town."

"You probably went to J. Colin English grade school, didn't you?"

"Yes, I did. You didn't go to the same school?"

"Off and on. We actually lived across the river most of the time. There were times when I stayed with Grandma and when I did, I went to your school. Time to ask: how old are you?"

"Thirty-eight. How old are you? Please tell me you're in your thirties."

Carrie giggled. "I'm thirty-six. The reason I asked was, we probably wouldn't have had much to do with each other in grade school, being two years apart. Then you would have gone on to North Fort Myers High School, right?"

"Right. I'm sure I would've noticed you for sure by the time you got to high school. And I don't remember you at all."

"That's because you were a Red Knight and I was a Green Wave. I went to Fort Myers High School. I spent a lot of time in the summers with my grandmother, but by the time I was in junior high and high school, I didn't need much supervision during the school year. I could take myself off to school in the morning and get myself home in the afternoons while my parents were working. So I didn't go to North Fort Myers at all."

"That explains it. You know, you sound as lonesome as I was. I was a latchkey kid, too." Shawn stuck the last French fry in her mouth.

"Oh, I don't know. I was lonesome, yes. I had friends, but back then, girls in junior high and high school were so cliquish. You know what I mean. If your older sister didn't know her older sister or cousin, or whatever, they didn't really want to talk to you. Besides, I was a bit bookish. I volunteered in the school library, so that made me a geek. I look back on that now, and remember happily helping out in the stacks, shelving books."

"Nice." Shawn smiled. "I was busy being crazy Shawn, playing softball and all that. But because I already knew I was gay and didn't make any real effort to hide who I was, I didn't have that many close friends other than Kelly in high school. Some girls wouldn't even be friends with me. I did hang out with some of the guys, even though I'm pretty sure most of them thought I was a bit weird. I was already living in a world of my own, writing stories and poems. Little did I know back then I would actually make a living from my writing someday. We never know where life will take us, do we?"

By the time they were leaving, the place was very busy and people were standing three-deep near the door waiting for tables. Shawn noticed Carrie didn't flinch when she put her hand in the small of her back on the way out the door. Shawn unlocked the Jeep and opened the door for Carrie, waiting for her to get in.

"You sure are polite," Carrie said to Shawn when she was back in the driver's seat.

"What do you mean?" Shawn reached to start the ignition.

"I mean, you didn't just click the door unlocked, you held the door for me. I can open a door. I'm not helpless. On the other hand, it was a sweet gesture."

"Oh, uh...well, thanks, I think." She chuckled softly. "As my mother used to say, I wasn't raised in a barn, although sometimes I might act like it."

A few minutes later, they stopped in front of Carrie's house. Carrie hopped out as soon as Shawn cut the ignition and motioned for Shawn to stay put. She came around to the driver's side of the Jeep, leaned in, and planted a short kiss on Shawn's cheek.

"Thanks for dinner," Shawn said.

"My pleasure. We'll have to do it again sometime. Anytime you want a dinner companion, just let me know. Catch you later." Carrie waved as she headed to her porch.

Shawn softly stroked her just-kissed cheek, backed her Jeep out of Carrie's driveway, and headed down the street to her own house, smiling all the way. *Take that, Jess! This neighborhood is looking nicer all the time*, she thought. Carrie was certainly more than she had bargained for when she saw her down the street. She'd be fun to hang around with.

CHAPTER NINE

A WEEK LATER, WITH a storm coming in the afternoon when she usually ran, Shawn decided to take her run early enough to get back ahead of it. On the way home, she saw a vehicle coming from the opposite direction. It slowed down and it appeared it was getting ready to turn into Carrie's driveway. After she got a better look at it, it was a pickup—obviously not Carrie's car. Now she was flat out feeling nosy about who was coming to Carrie's house when Carrie wasn't there.

The pickup turned into Carrie's driveway and she could hear it stop before she reached the front of the house. By the time Shawn was near the end of the driveway, still fairly hidden by the huge hibiscus bushes at the edge of Carrie's yard, the pickup door opened, and Jess got out. Since she hadn't been seen, Shawn decided to walk slowly past so she could casually look through the bushes and trees to see what was going on. The other pickup cab door opened, and there was Carrie. *Carrie? What was happening here?* Carrie leaned against the pickup, and Jess came around to her side. She leaned over and kissed Carrie like she was used to doing so.

Shawn felt the heat rise in her face and neck. She ran quickly past and away before anyone saw her. She couldn't get the scene out of her head, all of the time knowing she shouldn't have seen it. It was none of her business who Carrie saw or kissed. She shouldn't have been watching. She ran into her yard, stomped onto the porch, flopped down in the chair and sat there with her chin in her hands.

Carrie's my friend, and I was just spying on her. I feel like crap that I could do such a thing and I'll never do something like that again. Ever. Carrie can kiss whoever she likes. I just wish it hadn't been Jess.

***

Meanwhile, two doors down, Carrie quickly pulled away from the kiss. "Jess! What was that all about?"

Jess stepped back one step. "I thought...well, I guess I hoped anyway...you wanted me to kiss you."

"I'm sorry, Jess. I don't. I hope I didn't lead you to think otherwise. Come on, we've been through this. Let's just be friends. We've been friends for so long, I'd hate to lose you."

"You know I wish it could be more again. I wish I hadn't messed things up with us."

"Jess, think back. It wasn't just that. It wasn't working with us. The spark wasn't really there. I really like you, but please don't think we can be more than just friends. Very good friends, still just friends."

Jess looked into Carrie's eyes. "It's Shawn isn't it? You like Shawn, don't you?"

Carrie felt herself blushing and suddenly found her sandals interesting to look at. "I don't know yet. She's a friend right now and that's all there is. That has nothing to do with you and me. That us was over long before Shawn got here."

"I'd like to think that there's still something there, Carrie. We had a great time today. We still enjoy being together. I care about you." Jess stepped back further and put her hands in her shorts pockets.

Carrie looked back up at her. "I know, Jess. I care about you, too, as a friend. Please, let's keep it that way."

"Well, I hope it works out for you with your friend Shawn. If not, I'll be here. Waiting." Jess mumbled, "I hope she doesn't hurt you." She turned away quickly and strode to the driver's side of the pickup.

Carrie watched Jess drive away before turning and heading into the house. A short while later, she changed into her riding shorts. She pushed her bicycle out to the road shortly after five thirty, wondering what Shawn was doing.

CHAPTER TEN

SHAWN'S NEW OFFICE WAS coming along. She was starting to get excited about having someplace to work other than her lap or the kitchen table. Since seeing Carrie and Jess kissing, she'd gone back to running in the mornings and had avoided seeing Carrie at all. She knew what she had felt was pure jealousy even though she also knew she had no right to feel that way. She and Carrie weren't even dating. She attacked her work with a vengeance, figuring she'd wasted enough time on fun. That's what Carrie was, just fun. And fun time was over. She had work to do and a deadline to meet.

***

After a few more days, and no Shawn in sight, Carrie decided to go check on her. She could be sick, after all. Walking over to Shawn's house on Saturday, she noticed the sky was threatening rain. She could even smell rain in the air. Still, she figured she could get over there and back before it started. Coming up the driveway to Shawn's house, she could see the new addition taking shape. The footings for the bedroom and bathroom were in, as well as some of the studs.

Carrie saw Shawn's Jeep in the driveway. The woman was nowhere outside in the yard or sitting on the screened-in front porch, either. Carrie suddenly pictured Shawn sick; needing someone to take care of her, and hurried up to the front steps onto the porch, and knocked—no answer. Carrie looked around the front porch, at the two chairs they had been sitting in recently, enjoying margaritas and laughing. She sighed. She knocked again and waited.

Realizing she'd look pretty foolish if Shawn came running up the driveway, she cupped her hands around her face and tried to look through the front window anyway. There were no lights on and she didn't see anyone moving around. Maybe Shawn went out with someone else. Or she could be sick in there. *No, wait. The construction crew had been in there all week and they'd have noticed someone delirious. So she couldn't be in there sick. She was probably out. Still, why hadn't she at least come down to say hi? What happened to good neighbors?*

Carrie sighed, turned away, and headed back down the driveway. Although she told herself she didn't care what Shawn was doing or with whom, she couldn't help letting out a bit of disappointment by kicking at a few shells in the driveway on the way out. She tried to tell herself to quash that overactive imagination of hers, and remember that they were still just barely friends.

***

Shawn saw Carrie coming up the driveway. She couldn't shake the vision of her kissing Jess a few days ago, and for some reason it really bugged her. She needed to keep working. She heard her knocking but didn't answer and stayed in the kitchen working at the table until she was sure Carrie was walking away. That's when she noticed Carrie shuffling her feet in the shells in the driveway. Her shoulders were slumped, and she was walking slowly like she had something heavy on her mind. *I wonder what is bothering her. I really like her. Then why am I hiding in the kitchen. Pretty juvenile.* Starting to feel rather silly, she headed to the door to call Carrie back.

A sudden thunderclap made Shawn jump. Rain came pouring down as if someone quickly turned on a fire hose. Carrie had just reached the end of Shawn's driveway as Shawn ran to the door and called out to her. Carrie turned around, grinning from ear to ear, and came running back to Shawn's house and onto the front porch, already soaking wet.

"Oh, my God! I thought you were gone!" Carrie was breathing fast from running.

Shawn thought she looked adorable with rain dripping off everything in sight. *Oh, this could be trouble.* She looked away, trying not to stare.

"Uh, I was in the back, working." She tried not to stare at Carrie's nipples straining against the wet tank top. "You're soggy wet. Let me get you some towels and something dry for you to put on."

Although it was quite warm, goosebumps were forming on Carrie's arms. Thunderstorm rain was always cold. She wrapped her arms around herself as she stood on the porch dripping until Shawn came back with some towels. Stepping out of her flip-flops, she dried herself off enough to come into the house, leaving a puddle behind on the porch.

Meantime, Shawn went into the corner of the living room where her dresser now sat and looked for something dry Carrie could slip into. As she turned around holding a T-shirt and running shorts, Carrie stepped into the house with her own tank top and shorts adhered to every curve of her body. Shawn couldn't stop from looking at the unintentional display. Carrie blushed and wrapped the towel around herself.

"Sorry to stare, but you certainly do something for wet clothes." Shawn couldn't help smiling as she handed Carrie the dry things. "The bathroom is right around the corner. These things won't fit all that well, but at least they're dry. You can bring them back later. No rush."

"Thanks. I'm sure these will feel a ton better than what I have on right now. Any chance you might have a plastic bag I could toss my wet stuff into?"

Carrie followed Shawn into the kitchen where Shawn reached into a cabinet then handed her a plastic bag. She disappeared into the bathroom while Shawn poured two glasses of iced tea. By the time Carrie changed, Shawn was sitting in one of the two chairs left in the living room, with the cold drinks on the table between them.

"Come on, sit down. You might as well stay until the rain passes," Shawn said, pointing at the tea.

Carrie sat down, put the plastic bag on the floor and took a sip from her glass. "Excellent. You make wicked margaritas and great tea. Not bad."

"I can make do." Shawn grinned.

"So, what have you been up to, besides the remodeling going on?" Carrie waved her arm around at the construction zone. "I just realized this is the first time I've seen the inside of your house. I see you're sleeping in the living room. That must be fun."

"Yeah, I've been busy, all right. Deadline coming up and I'm not ready. This is the first time I've had a break all day other than stuffing something in my face a couple of times. A girl has to eat." She contemplated her iced tea glass.

"True. Still, don't you even run anymore?"

"Um, well, you know, it's getting warmer outside in the afternoons so I decided to run in the mornings, when it's at least a bit cooler. Clears my head for working."

"I came over to check on you because I hadn't seen you in a week or so. I was afraid you might be sick or something. You know, good neighbors and all that. Besides, I missed you."

"You did? For some reason I figured you were busy, or maybe you and Jess were going out...I mean in her boat or something," Shawn quickly added. "I figured you wouldn't miss me."

"Me and Jess? Nah. Remember I told you she's a good friend, and that's all there is between us."

Shawn thought for a moment while taking a sip of her tea. "I could've sworn I saw you with Jess in her truck a week or so ago when I passed your house. I guess I could've been wrong. She sure looked like Jess, though."

"Yeah, we did get a late lunch the other day. Ran into her and started talking, then decided to go get something to eat. That's all it was." Carrie blushed deeply. "Um...you didn't happen to see her trying to kiss me when she dropped me off, did you?"

Shawn felt the warmth rise in her face. "Okay, I confess. I did see Jess kissing you. I'm really sorry. I didn't mean to. I was running by when I happened to look down your driveway as I went past. It was none of my business and I shouldn't have been looking."

"That was all one-sided for sure. It was nothing, believe me. Hey, that's not why you haven't been around is it?"

"Well, a little part of it. I really did need to work. I saw Jess kiss you and I just assumed you were, um, busy." Shawn felt a huge lump form in her throat.

Carrie reached for Shawn's hand, holding it in both of her own. "Shawn, don't assume anything. Ask me. I know we're just friends, but that doesn't mean I'm not interested in more...I mean if you are. Maybe we should just get some things out in the open right now." Shawn looked up at Carrie, who took a deep breath. "Shawn, I like you. I'm attracted to you. You're fun to be with and you make me laugh. I'd like to see if this could go anywhere if you're interested."

Shawn felt the lump in her throat start to dissipate. "Wow...not what I was expecting to hear, thank goodness. I like you, too." She paused, looking straight into those brown eyes. "I don't know if I'm ready to be more than friends with anyone right now. It didn't work out well last time, and I just don't want to rush into anything. I'm just getting back to work, and it's something I have to do alone. And there are times I get on a marathon tear and barely come up for air, let alone another human being. I'm rambling aren't I?"

Carrie was grinning at her. "Would you mind very much if I kissed you?"

Shawn stood up, bringing Carrie with her. "No, I wouldn't mind very much at all."

Carrie leaned in and gently touched her lips to Shawn's. Carrie's lips were just as soft as Shawn imagined they would be, still tasting faintly of sweet tea.

"Again, please?" Carrie murmured.

Shawn obliged this time. She held Carrie's hands as she kissed her again. She could feel Carrie let go of her hands and melt into her arms, and deepen the kiss. Carries lips parted and their tongues explored. Carrie broke the kiss and pulled just inches away.

"Wow. That was some first kiss. And second kiss. " Carrie looked into Shawn's blue eyes.

"I could get used to kissing you," Shawn said, "That was very nice."

Carrie stepped back, reaching for Shawn's hand again. "Good start. Now, what do we do? How about we try spending more time together?"

"Okay. What would you like to do? Go out to dinner or a movie? Or would you rather go dancing somewhere?"

"First of all, let's agree not to go to the *Smokin' Pit* on a date anytime soon. Lunch maybe, with friends. If we can't live without their ribs or pulled pork one night we can always get takeout." Carrie chuckled. "Tell you what, how about I make some dinner at my house, since you're working so hard, and we could go out for a little dancing afterward? How does that sound? *The Lighthouse* is nice. It's out near the beach, but worth the drive."

Shawn grinned. "I think I like a take-charge woman. Sometimes. How about Friday? My book is due then, and I really need to buckle down. Once I get my manuscript sent in, I'll have more time for distractions for a while...meaning you. That is, until the edits have to be done."

"I distract you. All right, I like that. Okay, how about you come over at seven next Friday night. You aren't allergic to shellfish or anything like that are you? Just thought I should ask. Don't want to spend our first date night in the emergency room."

"Oh, no... nothing like that. I just hate pumpkin anything. Sounds un-American, doesn't it? I've never liked it. And mayonnaise. Don't like that, either. Other than that, I'll eat just about anything."

"All right, it's settled. I'll make supper for us. We'll talk before then? Oh, and by the way, casual attire is still good at The Lighthouse."

Carrie glanced over Shawn's shoulder toward the front door. "Hey the rain stopped. I need to get back home and let you return to work. I'd better go before I want to kiss you again." She laughed. "Too late." She planted another soft kiss quickly on Shawn's lips. Before Shawn could respond, Carrie scooped up her bag of wet clothes and headed for the porch.

Shawn was sure she had never looked as good in that T-shirt and those shorts as Carrie did. She was absolutely positive. She walked to the door, watched Carrie slip her feet into her flip-flops and head back toward her house. *Now that was an interesting rainstorm. And I'm in so much trouble.*

CHAPTER ELEVEN

THURSDAY NIGHT, CARRIE SETTLED in for the evening into the overstuffed chair next to the fireplace with a sigh and a book by her favorite romance novelist, S.K. Richardson. She'd read this book several times, but it was still her favorite. At the end of the book, the two main characters pledged their love to each other on a beach on Sanibel Island, at sunset of course. It was all just so romantic. All of S.K. Richardson's books were absolutely pure, unadulterated romance.

Even though Carrie knew it was one hundred percent fantasy, she compared every woman she'd dated to that fantasy ideal from those books. What's more, she assumed the writer who could come up with stories like that had to be the most romantic woman in the world. She had no idea what the author was really like, though, since she rarely did interviews. When she did those rare interviews, they were only about her books. Carrie sighed again and absently turned the book over. This one had a picture of the author on the back cover.

Carrie nearly dropped the book. The picture was of the author walking barefoot alone on a beach just before sunset, her hands in the pockets of her cargo shorts. She sure looked like Shawn, even though it wasn't a close-up. In fact, she looked enough like Shawn to be her or a twin sister. And so far, Shawn hadn't mentioned any twin sister.

It dawned on her that Shawn hadn't said what she was writing—just that she had a deadline. Rich said he thought she was a novelist, but he hadn't asked what kind of books she wrote. *Oh, my God*, she thought. *It can't be.* The short bio said the author lived in San Francisco. *Why haven't I noticed this before? I must have looked at this picture a dozen times. I just can't remember. I'm probably living down the street from my favorite author and even kissed her.* Her heart was racing. She jumped out of the chair and began pacing the room. *Now what?*

***

Following the last period in the paragraph, Shawn typed THE END. *Finally done!* She'd made one final tweak on the last page, and this book was finished. She e-mailed it off to AJ just after ten p.m. She turned off the lights and turned on the television, lying in bed with her back on pillows propped against the white wicker headboard.

She'd already replayed that kissing scene with Carrie in her head at least fifty times. She could feel the heat between them, and could still feel Carrie's touch on her hands and on her arm, not to mention on her lips. She knew she wanted more than kisses from Carrie. She also knew that was a dangerous road. Not necessarily with some women, but it would be with Carrie. She could tell Carrie was the kind of woman who wanted you to fall in love with her and ride off into the sunset. Well, she had already ridden off into the sunset once and look what happened— the sun came up the next day, the horse was gone, and so was the damsel. Shawn just wasn't sure she could do that again. Carrie was sweet and all that, and a great kisser. She had a very sexy body that Shawn would love to explore. She was also a lot of fun to hang around with. But—and this was a big but—Shawn wasn't ready to fall in love again. Yet. If she were ready, it would definitely be with someone like Carrie.

CHAPTER TWELVE

SHAWN TURNED DOWN HER driveway Friday morning after her run reliving those kisses from that stormy afternoon and the feel of Carrie's body against hers. And once again she felt like each kiss was attached directly to her core. She was feeling warmer by the minute, and it wasn't just from running. She needed to take a cold shower to get her mind off Carrie.

***

Carrie was reliving those kisses from just days ago. She was pretty sure she'd kissed her favorite author. Now she needed to find out if Shawn really was S.K. Richardson. There was only one way to find out for sure—ask her.

Carrie didn't want to be one of those silly groupies who yearned to be able to say she had kissed/slept with/dated someone well-known. S.K. Richardson was special because of the stories she wrote. Carrie wondered if it was true that it took a romantic to write them. Maybe it didn't. Well, tonight she'd make a nice supper for them and they'd go dancing and see what happened after that. If nothing else, she hoped they could be friends. If something more happened, that was a bonus.

For supper, she was planning popcorn shrimp, baked potatoes, and steamed broccoli with cheese sauce. And of course, there would be biscuits. She had a bottle of white wine ready and some iced tea, since they were going out. Maybe they'd drink the wine later.

At seven p.m. on the nose, Carrie heard Shawn coming up the driveway. By the time she opened the door, Shawn was stepping onto her porch with a bottle of wine in her hand.

"You definitely clean up well," Carrie teased her. She stepped back and waved her in.

"Not so bad yourself, either. You look really nice." Shawn stepped into the cool room, reaching out to hand over the wine.

Carrie took the bottle with one hand, then reached her other hand to Shawn's face and kissed her softly, barely grazing her lips. She hoped it would be enough to make her want more. Then she couldn't help coming back for a second, longer kiss, her lips parting for Shawn's tongue to briefly explore her mouth. This one made her knees start to buckle and the bottle of wine almost crash to the floor.

Carrie stepped back and took a deep breath. "Wow. To quote someone else from the other day, I think I could get used to kissing you." She took Shawn's hand and led her into the small dining area in the kitchen.

***

Shawn was nearly dizzy from that last kiss. She couldn't stop looking at Carrie. Her head was spinning from just being so close to her. The tantalizing aromas emanating from Carrie's kitchen made her stomach rumble, telling her that either she was starving or this was going to be one good meal. So now she could add "can cook" to the list of Carrie's positive attributes. Jen didn't cook worth a lick, and had no interest. Shawn had either done the cooking or they ate out. Of course there was always takeout. Carrie, however, was obviously very comfortable in the kitchen. Shawn opened the bottle of wine she had brought and poured each of them a glass before they sat down.

"A toast," Carrie said. "To us. To wherever this evening takes us."

"And to good neighbors." Shawn clinked her class to Carrie's, their eyes meeting over the top of the glasses briefly. "Thank you for making dinner. All of this sure looks good and smells wonderful. I haven't had a home cooked meal in a long time that I didn't make myself."

"You're welcome. I enjoyed making it. My grandmother always said feeding people you care about is a very wonderful thing, and I agree. She also said it was an art, if done well." Carrie grinned. "I don't know how artistic all of this is, but it's fun cooking for someone besides myself."

Shawn reached for a biscuit. "Well, it was very nice of you. Most of the women I've known have wanted to be wined and dined on a first date. And here you are, cooking for me."

Carrie reached for a biscuit at the same time Shawn did, their fingers touching for just a second as they reached for the same one. They both said 'go ahead' at the same time, too, then laughed. Shawn felt herself relax. She hadn't realized she was nervous until she began to breathe normally.

She was sure she showed considerable restraint in not heaping her plate, even though she was ravenous. "This is really good. So did your grandmother teach you to cook?" Shawn asked in between bites of cheese-covered broccoli.

Carrie smiled. "Yes, she did. Mom wasn't that great at it. I spent a lot of time with Grandma and she used to let me help her in the kitchen. Those are some of my happiest memories." She popped another shrimp in her mouth.

"That's so amazing. It's great that you have those wonderful memories and a very useful skill, as well. I never knew my grandparents. My mom was a late in life baby and her parents died when I was too young to remember them. My dad's parents died in an accident before my mom and dad got married. So what you had with your grandmother is very special. I'm glad you recognize how precious that is."

"I really do, believe me. All, right, then, what about you? You said you cooked too, so who taught you? Your mom?"

"Nope. Me." Shawn grinned.

"Seriously? You taught yourself?" Carrie put down her fork and put her elbows on the table, her chin in her hands. "How did that happen?"

"Starvation, actually. I never cared about learning anything in the kitchen when I was growing up. I was too busy doing other stuff, and my mom didn't really push me. Being an only child does help like that."

"Yes it does. I'm sorry you didn't have kitchen time with her. It's a great opportunity to talk and just be together."

"She was one of those who'd rather do it herself and I would've just been in the way. Once I was out on my own, I had to learn to cook or starve, since I couldn't afford to eat out all the time. So I went to the library, checked out a basic cookbook, and taught myself. Amazing what you can learn from books, isn't it?" She laughed. "I don't do anything fancy. It's sustenance cooking only, believe me. I can follow the directions on a frozen food package and make spaghetti and stuff like that." She grinned. "And I make great garlic bread."

"Garlic bread, huh? Do you make that for your dates?" Carrie leaned forward, grinning back. "Is luring them in with garlic bread a dating ploy for you?"

"Um...yeah...hey, I figured if both of us ate it, no big deal, right?" Shawn laughed as she found herself trying not to stare down the front of Carrie's blouse. She dipped another shrimp in cocktail sauce and popped it in her mouth to distract herself before picking up her fork again. "I've got an idea. Maybe I can teach you to make margaritas and you could teach me how to cook more things. Do you know how to make country fried steak? I love that stuff but always have to go to a restaurant to get it."

"Believe it or not, it's one of my specialties. I just don't make it very often because, well, it's not really that healthy. I'll admit it's delicious though." Carrie grinned again. "Tell you what, I'd be happy to exchange recipes and techniques with you. I'm sure we could learn from each other with some hands-on teaching. I'd love to learn to make margaritas."

"True, hands on is much easier. And much more fun." Shawn grinned back. "Maybe we could make a meal together some time and learn from each other. How does that sound?"

"I think that sounds like a deal to me."

After supper, they tidied up the kitchen. Carrie insisted they leave the dishes, saying they should get to The Lighthouse before it got so late there wouldn't be any tables left. The place was quite busy even during the off-season.

As Shawn drove to their destination, she looked over at Carrie, and found her looking back, smiling at her. Shawn reached over and took Carrie's hand in hers, stroking the back of Carrie's hand with her thumb absently as she drove. Looking back a couple of minutes later, she found Carrie almost staring at her with a quizzical look on her face.

"What's up?" Shawn squeezed Carrie's hand for a second before letting go.

Carrie blushed a little. "I was just wondering something."

"What would that be? Something I know the answer to, or one of those 'why is the sky blue' questions?" Shawn grinned and glanced back over at Carrie again before looking back at the road.

"Well, this might sound funny, but you look an awful lot like my favorite author. By any chance have you ever heard of S.K. Richardson?"

"Yes, I've heard of her." Shawn's stomach rolled over. She decided to keep it light and not assume anything.

"Has anyone ever told you that you look like her?"

"Yes, they have. Outstanding author and fine human being." Shawn barely glanced sideways at Carrie as her lips flirted with a smile. "From what I hear, of course. So, you're a fan of her books?"

"Sure am. I've read every single one she's written. I guess I just hope to meet Ms. Right and have a wonderful love affair like in one of her books. They're so romantic. I mean, who wouldn't want her sweetheart to make a declaration of love out on Sanibel Island beach at sunset? That's from my favorite book of hers, *Island Magic*."

"True, that does sound quite romantic. So that one is your favorite. What's your next favorite?"

Carrie thought for a few seconds. "*Second Chances*, I think. That one was actually pretty funny, as well as romantic. How many of her books have you read?

"All of them, actually," Shawn said softly. "I had to, since I wrote them." She kept her eyes glued to the road ahead.

"You really are S.K. Richardson?" Carrie stared at Shawn. "I don't think it actually occurred to me that you could be her until last night when I noticed you resembled the picture on the back of her—I mean your—book. I didn't even connect you. I knew you were a writer but it never occurred to me you could be her. Or she could be you. Or...oh, my God. Now I can say I kissed S.K. Richardson. How exciting!" Carrie paused and took a deep breath. "You know I'm kidding of course. I kissed Shawn Richards. So S.K. Richardson doesn't exist, does she?"

"Well, in a way, she does. She exists on paper. She exists on legal documents. As a real, flesh and warm-blooded person, no. She's kind of my alter ego. Like Iron Man or something." Shawn kept her eyes on the road, not sure what was coming next.

"I think I like Shawn Richards much better. You're real."

"Yes, I am." Shawn glanced back at Carrie, and then reached for her hand again. "Quite real." She felt she'd been holding her breath and could begin to breathe again. *Okay, that wasn't so bad*. They rode in companionable silence the rest of the way.

CHAPTER THIRTEEN

BY THE TIME THEY arrived, the popular hangout was already very busy. Shawn felt Carrie's hand reach for hers as they walked to the door. She liked that she could feel Carrie's hand was smaller than hers, but not tiny. Now that her secret identity was out, she was hoping Carrie didn't turn into another Jen. She and Carrie were pretty evenly matched in so many ways, with the easy give and take they shared quite comfortably. Carrie was fun to be with and they laughed a lot together. She was happy just to have her as a friend. Then she heard that voice in her head asking, *who are you kidding? You wanted to sleep with her the minute you first saw her. When was that? Was it just a few weeks ago?*

Shawn scanned the room looking for an empty table and found one just being vacated in the corner near the dance floor. She looked at Carrie for an okay before heading there with Carrie in tow. Once they were seated and drinks ordered, Shawn heard a song she liked and wouldn't trip over herself dancing to.

"Want to dance?" she asked, holding out her hand.

"I'd love to," Carrie said as she stood.

They found a spot on the dance floor and Carrie reached her arms up Shawn's shoulders to embrace her neck, her body in full contact with Shawn's. Shawn tried not to react as she felt every inch of her touch. As they danced slowly, her hands at Carrie's waist, Shawn realized how perfectly Carrie fit against her. How it felt like they'd been dancing together for their whole lives. How wonderful Carrie's hair smelled—a bit like coconut. And her fragrance—something clean like soap and water, yet sweet. She knew this was just a first date, yet it felt like something more. And that something more made her heart race and stomach clench at the same time.

Shawn pulled away from Carrie just a little bit so their bodies were not quite touching. She needed to put a little space between them. She wasn't ready to feel like that again about anyone. She didn't want to lead Carrie on, either, letting her think she could give her something she just couldn't.

Carrie looked up at Shawn. "Are you all right?"

"Uh, yeah, I'm fine. Just thought you might be uncomfortable." Shawn looked away.

"I'm good," Carrie said as the song ended and a fast song came on next. She backed away from Shawn about a step. "Hey, let's try a fast one."

Shawn seemed to relax a little as the music started and they began dancing again. She was so entranced watching Carrie's body move to the music, she almost forgot to move herself. Carrie seemed to have a natural feel for the rhythm and flow of the sound and went with it. Shawn would've been happy just watching her. They danced to several fast songs, laughing and singing along with the music. When the next slow one came on, they were ready to sit down.

"I love dancing," Carrie plopped into her chair with just a tiny sigh, looking out at the couples on the dance floor.

"You're a great dancer. It's been a while since I've danced with anyone, so I'm afraid I'm a little rusty."

"I'd never have guessed. You're pretty good yourself especially the slow dancing. I really enjoyed that," Carrie said, smiling softly and reaching for Shawn's hand. "You know, if you aren't comfortable with anything, all you have to do is say so. Did you feel uncomfortable slow dancing with me?"

"Maybe a little." Shawn squeezed Carrie's hand gently. "It's not your fault, it's just me. Besides, I like dancing with you so I'll get over it."

Their drinks arrived. They clinked their glasses as Shawn said, "To a fun evening."

"It already is," Carrie answered.

They sat out one song, watching the other couples dance as they sipped on their drinks. As another slow song started, Shawn put out her hand. "Want to try that again?"

Carrie nodded. "I'm up for it if you are."

Shawn led her to the dance floor, this time holding her close, but not too close. She felt Carrie's body in her arms, breathed in the fragrance of her hair once more, and almost lost track of the music. As that song ended she let go of her slowly and laughed a bit nervously as she reached for Carrie's hand for the fast song coming on. They danced several more numbers, afterward sitting down to sip on sodas this time, since Shawn was driving.

"This place is nice," Shawn said. "I don't remember it from when I was here last."

"It's sort of new. A couple of years old, but already very popular. I thought you'd like it, since they play a mixture of music, from oldies to current stuff."

Another song had started, so to be sure she could be heard Carrie leaned over, talking directly into Shawn's ear: "Hey, you want to go? I'm ready when you are."

Shawn could almost feel Carrie's lips touching her ear. The feel of her breathing on her earlobe nearly sent her into a tailspin. She managed to say, "Uh, yeah, I think I'm ready. Want to head back?"

Carrie nodded.

Shawn took Carrie's hand as they headed toward the door. Just before they reached the door, a voice called out, "Hey! Is that you Shawn?" Shawn dropped Carrie's hand and turned around just in time to find herself nearly nose to nose with a face she hadn't seen in years. Her face lit up with a huge grin.

"Kelly! You haven't changed a bit. How are you?" she said to a slightly taller and more substantial woman with short dark blonde hair, wearing cargo shorts and a T-shirt. They grabbed each other in a hug.

After Shawn released her, Kelly put her arm around Shawn's shoulders and said into Shawn's ear, "Obviously not as well as you are. Who's tonight's cutie?"

"Get outta here. I suppose I should make formal introductions. Kelly, I'd like you to meet my friend Carrie Alexander. Carrie, this character is an old friend of mine, Kelly Bradley. We haven't seen each other since…when?"

"I'd guess at least three years, maybe four. You'd never know it, of course. Shawn here never seems to change." Kelly looked appreciatively at Carrie. "And you, my dear, if you want to hear some Shawn stories, I could tell you some great ones. Like the time—"

Shawn cut her off. "Not now, Kelly." Shawn laughed. "I don't want to lose her as a friend when we're just getting to know each other. Maybe some other time. We do have to get going." She handed Kelly her cell. "Here, punch in your number. Let's get together in the next few days, lift a few, and catch up on stuff."

Kelly put in her number, and when she heard her own phone buzz in her pocket, she handed Shawn's phone back. "Let's make it soon. We've got a lot of catching up to do." She smiled at Carrie. "And nice to meet you, Carrie. I hope I get to see more of you."

Carrie reached out her hand to shake hands. Kelly took it and gallantly bent over, lightly kissing the back of her hand. "Till we meet again, fair lady," she said as Carrie blushed.

When Shawn and Carrie were back in the car and on the road, Carrie asked, "So you and Kelly have known each other a long time? Did you grow up together or something?"

"Or something. I'm not sure we actually grew up." Shawn shook her head, chuckling. "True story, we met in fifth grade. I was a little bit of a runt back then, and a bit too much of a tomboy for some of the kids in my class. The first time they picked on me, Kelly came to stand next to me and told them they could take on both of us at once. From that day on, she was my best friend. Kelly and I realized we both liked girls about the same time, and of course we came out to each other before even telling anyone else. She's always been more butch than I ever was, but she doesn't hold that against me." She paused. "Maybe that was more information than you were looking for?"

"Just curious. Is she always so gallant? You know, kissing hands and all that?"

"Oh…so she impressed you with that. Well, that's just Kelly. I think she sees herself as a knight in shining armor. Kind of a female Lancelot or something. I've used someone like her in several of my books as a main character. And she always gets the girl in the end. Whatever you do, don't tell her that. Her head would get bigger than it already is, and she'd probably want me to pay her part of my royalties if she knew."

"She probably would." Carrie giggled. "She didn't appear to be with anyone at The Lighthouse. Doesn't every knight have a damsel?"

"The last time I saw her she was with someone, but I don't know, now. Unfortunately, over time we sort of lost contact."

"How come?"

"My fault, totally," Shawn thought for a few seconds. "Jen, the woman I was with at that time, didn't care for Kelly, and it was mutual. I should've followed my nose right then and realized Jen wasn't right for me, but I didn't. Instead, I stopped talking to Kelly. I'm just glad she's talking to me again. Seeing me with you, she must have assumed it was over with Jen, since I hadn't told her."

"You guys do need some one-on-one time. I'm glad I got to meet her. She seems very nice. I already like her, and I'd like to get to know her better."

"Oh, you would, would you?" Shawn grinned as she started to reach for her phone. "Well, I've got her number here and maybe I could set you up with her if she's available. You did say you liked the characters in my books, and she's definitely a character. I'm pretty sure she likes you already."

"Very funny. She is cute, all the same."

"Well, just let me know if you're interested. Like I said, I have her number now." She patted the pocket of her shorts as if to reach for her cell again.

By then, Carrie was laughing pretty hard. "Cut that out," Carrie managed to say. "You're so funny. Kelly seems very nice, although I think I like you better. At least for right now," she teased back. "I was thinking more along the lines of a double date. Maybe we could go out together."

"Tell you what, I'll mention that when I talk to her. I'll bet she would like that."

They reached Carrie's house and the easy joking stopped as Shawn walked her up to the house. She could feel the tension rise as they stopped on the porch to unlock the door. Carrie wasn't quite ready for the evening to end as they went inside.

Shawn hadn't really noticed what Carrie's living room looked like earlier. That kiss last time had set her brain spinning. Now she looked around the living room and thought how much the room reflected Carrie. Comfortable, Old Florida style furniture, cane and wicker painted white, probably inherited from her grandmother. The cushions might've been recovered, but that was it. An antique oak table under the window facing the front yard had a double-headed lamp meant to be between the two chairs. The sofa was a comfy three-seater with a printed cover in shades of coral and green, with palm branches printed as a background. Like Shawn's house, this one had a small brick fireplace for chilly winter evenings.

"Would you like to stay for a glass of wine? We still have some left from dinner," Carrie offered. "Or I could make some coffee."

"Thanks, but I really should go. I enjoyed the evening with you. Maybe we could do something again soon. We could go out or I could cook something next time."

"That'd be nice. I'd like that," Carrie said. She stepped in closer to Shawn for a goodnight kiss. Shawn softly kissed Carrie, deepening the kiss when Carrie's lips parted. She backed Carrie up to the wall next to the front door as their bodies pressed together, the kiss becoming more urgent. Shawn's hands moved to cup Carrie's butt as Carrie's fingers threaded into Shawn's hair, urging the kisses on.

Shawn suddenly realized where things were headed, broke the kiss and backed away.

"I'm sorry. I don't know why I did that," Shawn said softly, looking away. Her hands in her shorts pockets said the evening had come to a screeching halt.

Carrie put one hand on Shawn's chest. "I'm not sorry at all. I liked it. A lot. If I didn't like what was happening I would've stopped it. Why do you think I encouraged you the way I did?"

"Um...I think I'd better go," Shawn said quickly, and without looking back at Carrie, she was out the door and into her Jeep.

Carrie watched Shawn's Jeep back out of the driveway. *Damn, if that was just a taste, wonder what it would be like to finish what we started*

CHAPTER FOURTEEN

A FEW DAYS LATER, Shawn and Kelly sat out on Shawn's front porch with cold Coronas on ice in a cooler and batter fried fish, French fries, and hush puppies from The Fish Fry.

"This is definitely hitting the spot. That Fish Fry bag sure brings back some fun memories. Thanks," Shawn said, stuffing another hush puppy into her mouth.

"Yeah, it does. All right, now give. What happened with you and Jen?" Kelly pulled the top off the takeout ketchup and dipped some fries.

"Well, I hate to say this, but you were right about her. She didn't really love me. She wanted me to be someone I'm not. Even though I tried very hard, I couldn't do it. All the socializing and all that she wanted to do just didn't leave me time to write. She was only happy when I was paying attention to her."

"Yeah, I could say something here. Being your friend, I won't."

"Go ahead, Kelly, say I told you so and get it over with."

"Okay, I told you so. You didn't hear it from me, though." Kelly grinned widely.

Shawn laughed. "You know, I've really missed you. You've always been a good friend and you know me better than just about anyone else. I should've realized that when you and Jen butted heads, it wasn't all your fault. Not that some of it wasn't, mind you."

Kelly nodded. "True, I'll admit some of it was me but most of it was her fault. She just wasn't right for you. How long has it been since you broke up?"

"It's been over a little over a year. Well, it was probably over long before that. She finally moved out when I was no longer entertaining enough for her. I stayed out there afterward, thinking maybe I belonged in California and that I could still write there. Hey, it was San Francisco, for crying out loud. I should've had all kinds of story fodder there. For some reason I didn't. I couldn't. I hardly went out and I wasn't writing very much. I pretty much wallowed in self-pity for a while. Probably much longer than I should have."

"What made you come home? How long have you been back?" Kelly reached for another piece of fish. "I don't know why, but I guess I always thought you'd eventually come back here."

"I've been back for about a month. I don't know what made me come back. I guess I just woke up one day and realized I wasn't where I wanted to be." Shawn took a swig from her beer bottle. "When I asked myself where I did want to be, there was only one answer—home. So one day I packed up everything, shipped some boxes back here, and with the rest packed into my Jeep, I drove back to Florida. Good thing it wasn't in the winter because I would've hated driving in snow."

"Well, you're back now. Just in time for hurricane season, too. I hope you'll stay this time. Hey, maybe you'll find some nice local girl and settle down. Speaking of...Carrie seems like a nice girl. Is she anyone serious?"

"You're the second person who has said that to me about finding a nice local girl and settling down. How funny. I don't know. I like her and she likes me. Anyway, I'm putting an addition on this house, so yeah, I'm staying this time."

"Well, that's a start..."

"Funny, she only lives two houses down. You can't really see much of the houses from each other. These places were built long enough ago and the trees and shrubs are so big that you can barely see the houses from the street unless you're standing practically at the end of the driveway. Good thing everyone here has mailboxes on the road with the numbers on them, or you'd never find anyone you were looking for."

"True, that's how I found you. Looks like you repainted the numbers on yours recently or at least it looks like you did. But back to Carrie..."

"As I said, I like her. We'd been running into each other in the afternoons after she gets off work. I was usually finishing a run about the time she started riding her bike. I noticed her, of course...who wouldn't."

"I definitely would've," Kelly said, grinning.

"Then we started talking a little bit in passing. I guess we really got to know each other better after I hired the company she works for to do my addition. The other night when we saw you was our first actual date."

"Aww…and I butted in. She wasn't swept away from you by my charms, was she?" Kelly grinned wider.

"Oh, I don't know, now. She did ask about you after we left."

"She did? What did she say?"

"I think maybe she was trying to figure out what my friends are like before she went out with me again. I'm pretty sure she already likes you, so that's good."

"Yeah? Well, let me know if it doesn't work out with you two and maybe I'll ask her out."

"Does that mean you aren't seeing anyone right now?"

"Yes, that's what it means. At least no one serious, just hanging out with friends. Let's see, I think I was with Sarah when we stopped talking. That was a long time ago. Sarah and I weren't that serious, though. We're still friends, but she's living with someone. Do you remember Andi Granger? That's who she's with. I'm happy for her. Anyway, there hasn't been anyone steady for any length of time since then. I'm just biding my time. The right woman is out there for me. I just know it."

Shawn reached into the cooler for another beer and handed one to Kelly. They both leaned their chairs back and propped their bare feet up on the porch rail. Shawn took a sip and gazed out at the front yard. "All right, how 'bout we talk about just that? How will you know when the right woman comes along?"

"I have a feeling I'll just know." Kelly stared at the top of her bottle.

"But how will you know? Do you have a list in your head of the perfect woman's attributes? I mean, knowing you and how much you like to eat, she'd have to be a good cook, for instance." Shawn chuckled.

"Very funny. I don't need a cook. I know my way around a kitchen, as you very well know," Kelly said. "Actually, I don't have a picture in my head. I just know I'll feel it in my heart. Yeah, I know I sound like someone who lives in one of those fairy tales you write, but seriously, I'll definitely know. What about you? Since we're now both convinced that Jen was not the woman for you, do you think you'll know when the right one does come along?"

"I guess so, but since I've already been burned, it'll be harder. I really like Carrie, but I'm nervous about getting too involved with her."

"Why?"

"She lives just down the street. What if it doesn't work out? Then we'd still probably see each other fairly often. It could be very uncomfortable."

"Well, I can imagine that would be. On the other hand, what if it does work out? What if she's the one? What then? You can't let what-if's ruin something before it even gets started."

"Yeah, I know. I'm not sure I'm ready to start something serious again right now. Carrie isn't someone you have a meaningless fling with. She's looking for her own knight in shining armor to love her forever. She wants to live out the romance novels she reads."

Kelly kicked Shawn's foot. "And look who writes those romance things."

"Okay, you're right. That's partly my fault because she loves my books and she wants to be romanced like that. She wants her 'happy ever after' like in one of my stories. I'm not sure I can deliver it in person. That's a lot of pressure."

"Hey, do you just think that stuff comes out of thin air into your brain? Well you my friend are the biggest romantic I've ever known. Don't you remember being so smitten with Tammy Brand in high school you wrote her poetry anonymously and put it through the louvers in her locker? Then there was Sheila Craft. You put a single rose on her front porch every Saturday night for a month until you realized her boyfriend was picking them up, tossing out the poems attached to them and giving them to her himself."

"Yeah, yeah. Well, that was then. Jen didn't care for love poems or single roses left with notes. I don't know what in the world I ever saw in her."

"I do," Kelly said. "She was gorgeous. She flattered you. She fed your ego for a while. You liked having her on your arm when you went out. As you know, that, my friend, doesn't last. There has to be more as you finally learned."

"Yeah, I know. I just don't feel like getting kicked in the teeth again. I want to be careful this time. I just...well, I guess I just want to be sure." Shawn took a deep breath and sighed. "Maybe I want to know for absolutely sure it's the real thing."

"Well, Carrie sure seems nice. She's very pretty. Even I can tell there's some intelligence behind those gorgeous eyes. Does she make you laugh?"

"Seems like we're always laughing about something."

"To me, laughing together is just about the most important thing. Not to get too nosey here, but how far has it gone with her?" Kelly asked quietly.

"Kisses. That's all. Wow, she's one great kisser! The first time I kissed her I wanted to keep on kissing her, but we stopped. The night of our first date, when we got back, I meant to just give her a little goodnight kiss, then it turned into more than that and I got scared and ran."

"Good grief. Did she act like she wanted you to stay?"

Shawn nodded.

"Then why did you run?"

"I don't know. I just suddenly felt out of control. I didn't want to do something we might not be ready for yet. She seemed disappointed when I backed away, but she was nice about it."

"Sounds to me like you're the only one not ready for something more." Kelly paused, tilting her head thoughtfully. "And she knows who you are now."

"Yes, she does. She didn't when we first got to know each other, though. She finally asked me the other night straight out. She saw that picture on the back of the one book I let them put my picture on and realized it looked a lot like me."

"Okay, then, at least you got to know her before she found out. She wasn't friends with you because you're some famous author. As you said, she liked you before she found out."

"Yes...she did."

"Well, that's something. You know this didn't get started like it did with Jen. Not the same thing at all. Even though I understand, you need to remember it's been a year. She's a very different woman, and this is an entirely different situation. You need to think of this as a new beginning."

"You definitely have a point. Or two, even. And I do appreciate the advice. I really do like her. Heck, she even wants to double date with you and your 'whoever.' What do you think? Do you have someone you can ask out? This might work better for me right now if we keep it on a lighter note with a foursome for dinner or something."

"Look, I've no problem with being your wingman on this. But you need to come to terms with how you feel about her."

"I know I do," Shawn looked down at the Corona in her hand. "We can't go on much longer like this."

"And she might not be patient forever. No one is that patient." Kelly stabbed her finger in the air toward Shawn as she spoke. "You could be relegated to friend status and never find out if she really is 'the one.'"

"I know that, too." Shawn let out a long sigh.

Kelly leaned back in her chair. "Well, if I were you, I'd ask her out again. Soon."

Shawn rolled her eyes. "I know, I know. I will."

"When?" Kelly pressed her.

Shawn looked over at her friend and smiled. "Tomorrow. I'll ask her out tomorrow for next Saturday night. How 'bout you, are you free?"

Kelly grinned. "Free-er than you are, buddy. I think you're smitten and don't even know it yet."

CHAPTER FIFTEEN

SHAWN WATCHED FOR CARRIE'S car to go by as she went home. She got out her bike, rode down the street past Carrie's house to be sure her car was there, and kept going. She'd planned to ride for a bit, before heading back about the time she thought Carrie might be starting out. By the time she rode down the street and around a couple of blocks and back, there was Carrie coming her way.

Shawn raised one hand in the nonchalant wave she had practiced, trying to look like she did this all the time and stopped by the side of the road waiting for Carrie to catch up.

"Well, look at you! Is that a new bicycle?" Carrie asked, grinning at her.

"Yep, it sure is. You inspired me to try riding as well as running. I'm still working on my skills and not quite up to a long ride yet. I'm getting there, though. Right now, just a few blocks at a time is all I'm doing, but it'd be fun to take a longer ride one of these days… maybe together?"

"Sure, whenever you think you're ready. I'll ride with you any time you like even on a shorter ride," Carrie said. "I enjoy going by myself, but it'd be great to have someone else along sometimes. By the way, I had fun the other night."

"So did I. In fact, I was thinking maybe we could go out again soon. I saw Kelly last night and I told her your idea about a double date. She said she liked that idea and left it up to us to decide when and where."

"I'd love to. When would you like to go? Friday or Saturday nights seem to work best for me. Either night this week is good."

"Great…how about Saturday night then? Are you up for maybe dinner out and then something else? I don't know what yet, we can work that out. Kelly might have some ideas, too, or if you do, just say so. Or maybe you like surprises?"

"I love most surprises. Well, not finding a snake in the house, but I'd imagine you wouldn't think that would be fun. So I'll leave that to you and Kelly. I'll wait to hear from you so I'll know what to wear that evening. How's that?"

"Sounds good." Shawn looked away then back at Carrie. "Listen, about the other night...I, um...I'm sorry I ran out like that."

"Not a total disaster. Really. Don't worry about it. We can talk about it sometime soon...maybe over a nice margarita on the front porch?"

"I would like that. Maybe tomorrow evening after dinner? Call me and I'll get it all set up if you're available."

"Will do. Well, I'd better get moving here. I've got a few miles to go this evening to work off a staff potluck luncheon. I'll call you tomorrow." Carrie pushed off on her bike and headed down the street, waving once before she turned the corner and out of sight.

Shawn stood and watched her go. Then got back on her bike and headed down the road toward her house. *Well, that wasn't too hard. A second date and this time it'll be a little less "date-ish" with another couple.* She turned into her driveway and pulled up in front of her house. *Another couple. I'm referring to us as a couple already. Don't panic Shawn, you'll survive. It's just a date. A going out and having fun kind of date. You'll be just fine.*

***

"So you asked her out already? Good job!" Kelly said when Shawn called her.

"Why does this feel so junior high school-ish? That's how I feel right now, like I'm back in junior high school asking a girl out. Good grief, we're nearly forty. At least this time I know the girl I'm asking out won't slap me. I guess that's something."

"True. Still, you were slapped by some of the prettiest girls in school. That's for sure."

"It would've been nicer if one of them had said yes, though. I didn't have any kind of idea that every girl in school wouldn't want to go out with me. I guess I had quite an inflated ego. Well, there were some lesbians in our school besides you and me, but they all seemed to be the wrong kind. I mean, nothing against us, but I don't want to date another you or another me."

"Yeah, me neither," Kelly agreed. "You know I'm not really that heavy into that butch/femme thing. On the other hand, I know what I like. And I like girls. Women, I mean. Ladies. Females who like being females. Not necessarily the dress wearing type, just the girly lingerie type under whatever they're wearing." She laughed. "Of course, you don't really know that until you get to know them better."

"Right you are. I'm guessing Carrie is the lingerie type, but I could be wrong. At this point, it's not something I really care about. She's a nice person and I enjoy her company."

"And kissing her. You like kissing her."

"And kissing her, true." Shawn sighed. "Okay, you go round up a date, and we need to figure out where to go. I told her we would come up with a surprise activity after supper."

"We'll work on it. Meantime, relax, will you? Take a deep breath, for crying out loud."

Shawn took an exaggerated deep breath so Kelly could hear her, and then laughed. "There, how's that?"

"Much better. Now, what's the next move?"

"I invited her over for margaritas tomorrow night. She likes my margaritas. We can just sit on the porch, sip a drink, and talk."

"Or not." Kelly obviously couldn't help laughing.

"No 'or not' tomorrow. Just a nice quiet evening sitting on the porch like neighbors, imbibing alcoholic drinks, and talking. That's it."

CHAPTER SIXTEEN

SHAWN WAS BUSY MIXING up a batch of margaritas when Carrie appeared at the front door. She looked up just in time to hear her holler.

"Hey Shawn! You back there?"

"Be right there. Take a seat out on the porch and I'll bring us some of this concoction."

"Bring the pitcher," Carrie called back.

Shawn brought out two margarita glasses along with a good-sized pitcher of strawberry margaritas.

"I hope you don't mind. I put strawberries in them for something different." She set the glasses down and began to pour the frozen pink confection into them.

"Mind? No, not at all. I love strawberries." Carrie lifted her glass. "So what shall we toast tonight? It seems a shame not to toast something with these great drinks in front of us."

"Well, let's see. We could toast today being Wednesday. We could toast it not raining. We could toast surviving our first date and still being friends."

"Let's do that. We went on our first date and we're still friends. I like it. Here's to first dates," she said. She took a sip. "I like this! And here's to the next date. "

"Agreed," Shawn said, sipping her drink. "I'm glad you like these. I like to try different things, and strawberries were easy. In a bar I went to once in San Francisco, there was a whole menu of different flavors of margaritas. Their specialties were flavors like watermelon, peach, strawberry, mango, and the like. There was some exotic stuff, too, but all I can remember now were cucumber and wasabi flavors. Most of them sounded kind of gross, but some of my friends thought they were great."

"You know, I think I would like California," Carrie said, gazing out into the yard. "I've never been there, but you always hear things about how it is.

"California isn't all it's cracked up to be. It really isn't." She shook her head slowly.

"What do you mean? Didn't you like it?"

"Oh, don't get me wrong, it's pretty nice. In some places there are a lot more people who live their lives and don't worry about what other people think. It's almost like there are two different states within one. Or maybe even three."

"Want to explain?"

"Well, there's the whole LA thing. It's basically a desert with water piped in. You know, palm trees, Rodeo Drive, Beverly Hills, the whole movie star thing, and of course Disneyland."

"That's what I always think of when I think of California. Well, except for Disneyland. We have Disney World here, so…"

"I guess that's probably true of most people, because of all the movies and TV shows. I think that's what I had in mind when I went there the first time. But then there's the Bay Area, including San Francisco and the area around it. Totally different kind of place. Cool, foggy, and hilly. They don't usually need an air conditioner there. Not at all like LA, where they run their air conditioning most of the year. Then there's most of the rest of the state north of LA, which is mostly agricultural. You know, county fairs, acres of crops, and cows and all that. Of course, there are also the mountains, where the skiing is outstanding unless there's a drought. I guess that makes four places, but it's a lot of different places in one state, that's for sure."

"But you don't live there anymore. Besides the fact that you had a nasty breakup, you still moved away from the whole state. Why?"

"California isn't Florida. I think I always knew it wasn't really home. Want to hear something funny? If you tell a Californian you're moving to Florida, they ask if you aren't worried about hurricanes, especially if you're moving out here anywhere near hurricane season. If you tell a Floridian that you're moving to California, they ask if you aren't worried about earthquakes. You haven't asked me about the earthquakes."

"Well, I think everyone has heard about earthquakes in San Francisco, especially that one during the World Series. Isn't San Francisco supposed to fall off California and into the Pacific someday?" Carrie laughed. "Just kidding. But seriously, wouldn't you rather take your chances with a hurricane than an earthquake?"

"I would. At least you know a hurricane is coming and can do something about it…like either get supplies together and ride it out or get out of the way if you can't. Earthquakes…well you never know they're coming and they just happen. There's no radar for them. I prefer dealing with hurricanes for sure."

"Me, too." Carrie looked serious. "I have a hurricane kit at my house, including a generator. All the generator needs is gas, which I get if I see something even remotely heading this way. The last time it happened, I ended up not having to buy gas for my car for a month when one storm veered away. Better that, though, than being in long lines at the last minute."

"Smart girl. I need to get mine together, too. I used to own a generator, but I sold it when I left here for California. I figured someone else could use it and it shouldn't just sit there rotting when I wasn't here. I gave a young couple a great deal on it. I suppose I should get another one now that I'm back."

"BJ's has them at a decent price. The only trick is getting it home, since it would be a real pain, if not impossible, to try to fit it into your Jeep. A friend of mine from work helped me get mine home in his pickup to save me the delivery charges. If you need help, let me know. I'm sure he'd help you pick it up, too," Carrie offered.

"Thanks, I'll keep that in mind. Another margarita? We don't want them to melt, do we?"

An hour later, the margaritas long gone, Carrie rose to go. Shawn got up, too. "How about I walk you home?"

"Why, how gallant of you! Are you competing with Kelly for Chief Knight in Shining Armor?"

"Well, I hadn't thought of that, but maybe I should." Shawn laughed as she slid her feet into her flip-flops. "Actually, I could use a little exercise, and I'd feel better knowing you got home safe. Sometimes I think this place needs some street lights."

"Street lights? Nah. I like living out here. It's sort of like living in the country. In town, you'd have a much smaller lot, and no nice big, long driveway you can turn around in."

"Very true. Let's walk." Shawn took Carrie's hand as they headed down Shawn's driveway. They strolled down the short distance between their houses and then up Carrie's driveway. Their flip-flops made crunching noises on the driveway as they walked in silence, barely looking at each other.

Shawn's hand tightened around Carrie's and then let go as they got to the door. She waited as Carrie unlocked her door and stepped inside.

Carrie took Shawn's hand again and pulled her inside as well.

"I really can't stay…"

Carrie pushed the door shut behind them, pulled Shawn close and kissed her gently. "See, that wasn't so bad, was it? I like kissing you. This was just a goodnight kiss."

"I do like kissing you, too. I like you very much. I just…I just, well, I need to go slow." Shawn paused, looking at those pretty eyes. And those long eyelashes. And those soft lips that wanted to be kissed. She gulped in some air. "Forgot to tell you, Kelly has found herself a date for Saturday night, and we were thinking it'd be fun to run out to Fort Myers Beach. There are tons of places to eat out there, and then we could find something to do on the beach, I'm sure. My cousin has lived there for years and knows all the fun places to go. Unless you have someplace in mind you'd like to go, I'll call him."

If Carrie noticed the change in subject, she didn't let on. "That sounds like fun. No, nothing particular comes to mind. I'm looking forward to it. So casual attire, shorts even?"

"Sure. Let's be comfortable. How about if I come get you about seven, then we can go pick up Kelly and her date and head out? Does that work for you? It can be earlier or later if you like. Doesn't matter to me. Just need to let Kelly know what time we're picking them up."

"I like seven. That sounds like we'll be out at the beach early enough to watch the sunset after we have dinner. I'm looking forward to it."

"Me, too. I better get going. If I don't see you before, I'll see you Saturday evening then." Shawn took Carrie's hand and pulled her closer. Another goodnight kiss was in order. Another soft kiss brushed against Carrie's lips, a whispered goodnight and Shawn was out the door. She waved as she made her way down Carrie's driveway.

***

Carrie watched Shawn stride down her drive and could hear her steps even after she was out of the pool of light thrown by her porch light. The porch light was on a motion sensor and finally turned off a few minutes after Shawn left the yard. Carrie realized she was still standing on her porch in the dark and went inside. This Shawn was something else—a cross between a golden knight and a teenager. Shy but bold at the same time. Sometimes Carrie could feel Shawn wanting her, gazing at her with those blue eyes that seemed to see right through her. But at other times, she seemed like some kind of scared kid that had been slapped too many times or was afraid of thunder.

Shawn Richards was an enigma for sure. Carrie had already decided she was going to be patient and see where this went. One kiss was all it took and she was toast. She could feel the heat between them every time they accidentally touched and especially when they kissed. Even that soft brush of a kiss was enough to set her on fire. She wanted more. She wanted way more.

Carrie imagined them coming back to her house on Saturday night, after a night at the beach. They would get out of the car, walk up to the door, she'd bring Shawn inside. Then she'd kiss her brains out and throw her down on the sofa and make mad passionate love to her. Yeah right. No, that's not quite the right scenario. Try again.

Okay, how about they come back from the beach, come in the door, and she offers Shawn a glass of wine as they sit on the floor cushions and listen to music. They get carried away by the music and wind up making love on the floor. Not quite right. She decided to consult one of those S.K. Richardson novels for some ideas. Somehow, she so wanted to touch Shawn, to make love to her. To feel her skin to skin. To taste her all over. Oh yeah, that's what she wanted, all right. She had a good idea that's what Shawn wanted, too. But what kind of scenario to play that out in? How could she get Shawn to just relax and let it happen?

Whoever made Shawn so gun-shy really did a job on her, she thought. Carrie already knew she cared very much about Shawn and wanted her to be part of her life. Before anything else could happen, though, she needed to get her to relax after the first kiss. The other night when she pushed her up against the wall, Carrie was sure it was going to happen then. She was trying everything she could to let her know she wanted it, too. But then she ran off. Carrie wanted the rest of it. And she wanted it from Shawn.

She knew she had a romance novel idea of love playing around in her head, but she also knew that Shawn could be the one she was looking for. Every time she looked into her eyes she could feel that Shawn felt something, too. But if she couldn't get her to do something about it, they could be doomed before they really even got started.

CHAPTER SEVENTEEN

SATURDAY EVENING. SHAWN HAD three pairs of cargo shorts laid out on her bed, trying to decide what to wear. She had sleeveless tops, polo shirts, and even a couple of nice tank tops laid out playing mix and match with them. She moved the blue polo shirt over with the tan shorts. Then moved the turquoise top onto the white shorts, then the navy top over with the yellow shorts. She finally settled on the navy blue polo shirt with the stone colored shorts. She put them on and stood in front of the wall mirror she had propped up in the living room.

Okay Shawn, you don't look half bad, she told herself. The navy blue looked good with her blonde hair and blue eyes. The shorts were a good length and hid the whitest part of her legs. She slipped on some brown sandals. Good outfit. Sliding her wallet into her pocket, she picked up her keys and headed for the Jeep. She looked once more at herself in the rearview mirror. *Enough, Shawn. You're starting to act like some kind of narcissist, worrying so much about how you look.* She started the Jeep and once more repeated it's just a date. It's just a date. *I really like her. But it's just a date. Relax.*

Carrie was already dressed and ready, trying not to stand by the door to watch for Shawn to come down the driveway. She had already checked how she looked several times. She had changed outfits several times as well. She wanted to make sure she looked nice, but casual. Sort of sexy but not enough to scare Shawn. A final check in the mirror showed the navy shorts and a pale yellow sleeveless blouse did her justice.

As soon as Shawn turned down Carrie's driveway, she saw her on the porch, already locking the house door. By the time Shawn pulled up, she had walked out to the driveway. She motioned for Shawn to stay in the Jeep and slid into the passenger seat.

"Wow...you really look great tonight," Shawn said. "I mean, you look nice all the time, but you look especially nice tonight."

"Thanks so do you." Carrie reached over and kissed Shawn lightly on her lips. "I'm looking forward to this evening."

Shawn felt her insides instantly turn to mush, but tried to ignore it. "Me too."

As they drove over to Kelly's, Shawn felt Carrie's hand touching hers and looked over to see Carrie smiling back at her. She smiled back and took Carrie's hand. *That wasn't very hard. We've done that before.* Except this time Carrie's touch sent electric shocks up her arm that led to other parts of her body that she shouldn't be thinking about right then. She squeezed Carrie's hand and kept driving.

A bit later, they were standing around with Kelly in her front yard, waiting for the last member of their foursome to arrive. "Yeah, I know she's late," Kelly said. "Not a good start, but she did call. She said she had to work a little late and will be here in a few. Y'all might as well come on inside while we wait. Carrie, you look great, by the way."

"Thanks, Kelly," Carrie said as they stepped inside. "Nice place. Have you lived here long?"

"A couple of years. This is my second house. I sold the first one after I fixed it up and made enough money for a nice down payment on this one. Now I'm renovating this one. It's sort of a hobby." Kelly pulled out her phone and thumbed through some photos. "Want to see?"

"Sure, I'd love to."

"This is what this house looked like before, and you can see the after."

"Wow. You could definitely do this for a living if you wanted to. If you're ever looking for a job, let me know. I work for a construction company, and renovations and additions are part of what we do. My boss is always looking for talent, and you definitely qualify there."

"I love doing this for myself, but I'm not sure how much I'd like doing a job for someone else. Working on my own house, I can take my time and decide exactly what I think it should look like. If I did this work for someone else, it'd be their idea of what should be done. I guess I could do that if I had to, but I don't think it would be near as much fun. Doing it for myself is relaxing."

The sound of the doorbell startled everyone, making them laugh. Kelly's date was a cute redhead in her early thirties with freckles all over her face and arms. Kelly hugged her briefly and brought her in to meet everyone. "Shawn and Carrie, this is my friend Tracy Creamer. She's a photographer."

Carrie reached out to shake hands. "A photographer...what an interesting profession. Are you a wedding photographer, portraits, or wildlife, or…?"

"Actually, I do a little of everything. Whatever strikes my fancy. I prefer pictures of wildlife or the outdoors, but I pay the bills by doing portraits at Edison Mall. It isn't a bad gig. Most people are very nice and are excited about having their pictures taken for a family event or birthday."

"Doesn't sound bad at all to me," Shawn said. "Creamer. Sounds familiar. Have you ever shown your work in San Francisco?"

"Actually, yes, I have. I had a showing just once a couple of years ago. It wasn't in a fancy gallery, though it was well reviewed and I did sell some prints there."

"I own one of them," Shawn said. "I bought the photo taken on a Captiva Island beach with a sandpiper on it and a worn down piece of beach fence. I was pretty sure I knew exactly where you took it. At the time I bought it, I was homesick and that picture gave me a piece of home there."

"Well, thank you. I'm glad you liked it. So that picture lives in California?"

"Oh no, that photograph came back here with me. I wouldn't leave it behind. It's hanging on my wall here."

"Okay enough shop talk. Let's go get some food. I'm starving," Kelly said.

"Do we know where we're going for supper? I'm definitely curious what you two came up with." Carrie looked from Shawn to Kelly for an answer.

"Well, my cousin recommended a fairly new place called the Yucatan Beach Stand," Shawn said. "I told him we wanted to keep it casual. He swears it's an actual sit-down place. They have great food, and you're inside and outside at the same time. It's not right on the beach, but close to it, so maybe we can walk on the beach later."

"That sounds like fun," Tracy said.

"I'm with Kelly," Carrie said. "Let's get going."

CHAPTER EIGHTEEN

AS THEY DROVE OVER the bridge into Fort Myers Beach, the crowds on foot became more pronounced. People were walking around all over, in various stages of attire – from swimsuits to dresses. Just the parade of humanity was entertaining. Shawn turned right just after the bridge and found the Yucatan Beach Stand right where her cousin had described. The parking lot seemed to be full. They could hear a steel drum band playing as they finally found one spot left in the parking lot and slid the Jeep into it, being thankful for not having a large vehicle.

The restaurant looked like something out of a movie. It had a palm frond thatched roof, woven bamboo half-walls all around the outside, and bamboo blinds rolled up for the evening. Since it was still quite warm, it appeared everyone who was already there was claiming seats along the perimeter to watch the human parade go by.

Just as they gave their names to wait for seating, a table came open at the outside so they took it. Carrie felt Shawn's hand on her back and her arm halfway around her as they followed the waiter to their table. Even after they sat down on the high stools at the well-polished wooden tables, Carrie could still feel Shawn's touch. She knew her hand was no longer there, but she could still feel its warmth.

Carrie tried to make small talk during dinner, but all she could think about was walking down the beach at sunset, hand in hand with Shawn. The possibility of that happening was pretty slim, but a girl can have her fantasies, can't she? She could see them kicking off their sandals and carrying them, their feet making little toe prints in the damp sand. Maybe they would wade in the little waves by the shore, looking into each other's eyes off and on. Then Shawn would put her arm around her and kiss her. Yes, that would be very nice.

"Carrie, what do you think about that?" Kelly asked.

"Uh, what?" Carrie suddenly realized she had no idea what she was being asked about.

Shawn laughed. "You were a million miles away. That was pretty obvious. This beach air making you dreamy?"

"I guess that's it. Sorry. I didn't mean to zone out on you guys."

"That's okay. We were just wondering how your grouper is. You were the only one who ordered it. It looked good," Tracy said.

"Oh. Yes. The grouper. It's really great. How are the scallops, Tracy?"

"Love them. Looks like Kelly liked them, too. The operative word here being liked. Hers are already gone. So are Shawn's shrimp. Guess we owe your cousin a thank you for telling us about this place, Shawn."

"I agree," Shawn said. "The service is good, too. I'll call him tomorrow and thank him."

"No, call him now," Carrie said. "We should tell him we're having a great time and thank him."

"Okay. Let's do it." Shawn pulled out her phone and punched in Greg's number.

"Shawn! Everything going well?" Greg asked. They could hear a band playing in the background.

"We're fine. Actually, we're enjoying our dinner so much we decided to call right away to thank you for recommending this place. I warn you we have you on speaker so don't say anything you'll regret later." Shawn chuckled. "Sounds like you're having a good time yourself, so we won't keep you."

"Hey, that's great! I'm glad you guys are having a great time. In fact, I'm just down the street from you if y'all want to come. I'm at the Bait Bucket having a drink. You can park down the street at the public parking and walk down here. There's a great band playing. You could even sit on the beach to listen to them."

"We might just do that." Shawn looked around the table and everyone nodded yes. "Make that we will do that. See you in a little bit. One of us is a little slow finishing her dinner," she looked pointedly at Carrie.

Carrie began stuffing food into her mouth like a cartoon character, making the rest of them laugh. It didn't take long for them to head out to the car and on to their next big adventure. The surprise this evening turned out to be on all of them, since none of them had ever been to the Bait Bucket before. They were sure it was not a gay/lesbian place, so they would not be dancing, but it would be fun to have a drink and enjoy the music for a little while.

Greg had a second table pulled over next to his when they got there, with some extra chairs so they could all sit together. Shawn introduced her party to Greg, who shook each hand as he was introduced.

No introduction was necessary for one member of the party. "Carrie, so nice to see you again," Greg said. "Always a pleasure."

He looked at Tracy a second time when introduced and then asked, "I hope you won't be offended, but you wouldn't be a photographer, would you? I own a really nice print by a photographer by the same name."

"I'm not offended at all. I am a photographer. If you'll describe the picture, I'll tell you if it's mine."

"It's the one with a seagull standing next to a single conch shell that looks like it washed up on the beach."

"That's mine," Tracy said, smiling. "I like that one, too. You must've gotten that one a while back, since I haven't made a print of it for several years."

"A few. It's definitely one of my favorites. I have it in a sixteen by twenty matted in a twenty by twenty-four frame that looks like driftwood. It's beautiful. Have the rest of you seen any of her work? It's great."

"Shawn said she has one of her pictures, too," Carrie volunteered.

"Yes, I do. Tracy is quite talented." Shawn nodded in Tracy's direction and smiled.

"Well, you guys are really great for my ego, that's for sure. Now if I could just get the rest of the world to see how great I am." Tracy chuckled. "I could quit my day job at Picture World in the mall."

"Keep at it, Tracy. You have talent, that's for sure. Now, how about a round of something to drink here? My treat," Greg said.

As they went around the table ordering drinks, Carrie realized she might be a little out of her element with this group. Carrie suddenly felt a little insecure and a bit jealous. Greg owned his own IT company, Shawn was a well-known writer, Kelly renovated houses for fun, and Tracy was a photographer. Carrie knew she didn't have any kind of talent like that. She suddenly saw herself as just an office worker. Not that she wasn't a valued person to her boss. She knew she was and she also knew she was good at what she did. Still, she didn't have any kind of talent like the others. Then she found out Shawn and Greg each had one of Tracy's pictures on their walls.

As their drinks arrived, the waiter put her and Shawn's drinks down next to each other. They both reached for them at the same time, their hands touched just for a second, and Carrie felt something akin to a leap of fire from Shawn to her. They both must have felt it at the same time, because they both looked up and into each other's eyes immediately.

Carrie was sure Shawn felt it, and when Shawn squeezed her hand her suspicion was confirmed. But when Shawn went right back into the conversation, she thought maybe it wasn't what she thought. Shawn's eyes didn't betray anything when she looked up at her. Just the friendly smile Carrie always saw.

***

Greg watched the interaction between his cousin and Carrie. *Well, well...what do you know? Not just a friend. Shawn had said she was just looking for someplace to take some friends out for a fun dinner at the beach. She didn't mention anything about a girlfriend*

"Carrie, would you care to dance with me?" Greg asked when the next song started.

"I'd love to," Carrie said, glancing at Shawn, who just smiled back.

Greg noticed Shawn's eyes were glued to Carrie as he led her out to the dance floor for a slow dance. He kept her at some length away. All the same, he could tell Shawn couldn't stop watching.

"So Carrie, are you and Shawn serious?" Greg asked.

"Well, you'd have to ask her. I'd like it to be serious, but to tell you the truth this is only our second real date."

"Really? Just watching the two of you, one would think it was farther along than that. My cousin is a little gun-shy currently, but you probably already know that."

"I do know," Carrie sighed. "I couldn't help noticing. I really like her a lot. You two seem very close. Got any suggestions?"

"Just hang in there. I'd say she really likes you too, from what I can see. She doesn't give her heart easily. The last time she did, it got stomped on pretty hard. She won't want to take a chance on having that happen again right away. She's one of the most wonderful people I've ever known, even if she is my own cousin. She just needs kid gloves right now."

"Thanks Greg. I really am trying."

***

Shawn watched them dancing and chatting like old friends out on the dance floor. She would've given anything to find out what they were talking about, but she knew she wouldn't ask. She also wished she was the one holding Carrie and dancing with her.

Just then she noticed a couple of women dancing together. No one seemed to notice or care, and the floor was fairly crowded. Just as Shawn decided to get up and cut in on her cousin and Carrie, the song ended and the band took a break. Carrie and Greg came back to the table, Greg with Carrie on his arm.

"See, I brought her back. I saw you watching us. Did you think I was going to try to run away with her?" Greg swatted Shawn on the shoulder like they had done when they were kids.

"I guess that would've been up to Carrie, now, wouldn't it?" Shawn swatted him back as Carrie took her seat next to Shawn.

Greg leaned over to Shawn. "I like her. And guess what, she really likes you."

"Yeah, I know. I like her too," Shawn said. "I just…"

"Well, don't 'I just' too long, girl, or you might find yourself alone. She's sweet and very pretty. You can bet we aren't the only ones in the world who've noticed that, either."

"I know, I know."

Shawn turned around and put her arm across the back of Carrie's chair. She leaned in and whispered to Carrie, "Greg likes you."

"I like him, too. Since I worked with him on our computer system, I already knew how nice he is. He sure cares a lot for you. Have you always been very close?"

"Since I was little. He's ten years older than I am, but you would never know it to look at him, would you?" They both turned and looked at Greg at the same time.

"What?" he said.

"Nothing," Carrie and Shawn said in unison, and then laughed. Shawn's arm moved to around Carrie's shoulders seemingly of its own accord and stayed there.

***

Carrie leaned into Shawn's closeness and smiled as she enjoyed every minute of it. She breathed in Shawn's fragrance of green tea and lemon grass. *Clean and yet sexy. Sweet but yet … something.* She felt she could drown in it, yet didn't feel like drowning. She wanted to nuzzle her neck. She wanted to…do inappropriate things in a straight bar and right in front of Shawn's friend and Shawn's cousin. Heady with Shawn's nearness, she could feel herself getting quite warm and damp and decided she needed to make a trip to the ladies' room. She excused herself and Tracy got up to accompany her. Minutes later, they were in the women's room, standing in front of the mirror brushing their hair.

"So how long have you known Shawn? She seems very nice. She's definitely cute."

"Not long. Just a month or so. How long have you known Kelly?"

"Same. Just a month or so. Are you and Shawn a couple or just friends?" Carrie noticed Tracy glance at her in the mirror as she returned her brush to her bag.

"We're just friends, pretty much. We're also neighbors. I live just down the street from her." Carrie picked up her bag. "What about you and Kelly...anything serious there?"

"No, just good friends." Tracy winked at Carrie. "With benefits, if you know what I mean. So you and Shawn aren't involved? I mean, if I asked her out, you wouldn't mind?"

Carrie felt a sick feeling form in the pit of her stomach. "Well, I'd say that's up to Shawn. We've only been out a couple of times. I don't think anyone could say we have any claim on each other at this point. Anyway, she stays pretty busy with her writing."

"You know, they say all work and no play..." Tracy laughed and tossed her auburn curls. She put her arm through Carrie's like they were old buddies, and they went out the ladies' room door together.

As they walked back to the table, Carrie played with the idea of socking Tracy in the mouth or yanking out some of that red hair. Just as suddenly she felt pretty silly about both options. She and Shawn had nothing exclusive going on. If Shawn wanted to date Tracy, it was her right. But maybe, Carrie decided, she needed to give Tracy a run for her money.

Carrie sat back down beside Shawn and pulled her chair a little closer to Shawn's and whispered in her ear, "Did you miss me?" After Shawn grinned back at her, Carrie glanced over at Tracy, who smiled back, raised eyebrow in response.

***

Shawn caught the short exchange between Carrie and Tracy out of the corner of her eye and wondered what was going on. Whatever it was, she decided it couldn't possibly have anything to do with her, so she let it go.

"You up for a walk on the beach?" Shawn asked, looking at Carrie.

"A sunset walk on the sand sounds like a great idea."

Shawn looked at Kelly and Tracy. "What do you think? You guys up for it?"

A few minutes later, sandals in hand, the four of them were strolling barefoot in the sugary sand, still warm from the day's sun, the outgoing tide lapping softly at their feet. Even without touching, Shawn could feel Carrie close to her and heard her talking about something, but barely heard what she said. Every time she looked over at her, Carrie's face appeared to be lit from the sunset, making her look like some kind of golden goddess with her hair moving in the evening sea breeze. She had to look away to breathe.

"Hey Shawn," Kelly called out from behind them. "You guys go on ahead. We'll sit here and catch you on your way back, okay?"

Shawn waved at her in response, reached for Carrie's hand, holding it tightly for a few seconds as Carrie smiled at her, before letting their clasped hands drop between them. As the sunset deepened they passed the wide public beach area in silence and strolled farther to where the beach scrub came within a few yards of the waves. Realizing they were nearly alone finally, they stopped.

"Shawn?"

Shawn realized Carrie had caught her staring at her. "You look beautiful tonight." Golden goddess Carrie smiled back at her and Shawn realized she had been holding her breath. Without thinking, her hand stroked Carrie's cheek and she softly kissed the goddess' yielding lips. She felt a sensation of floating. She shook her head in an attempt to clear it, turned them around, and headed back up the beach.

***

Later, as they drove back to Kelly's, Tracy asked Shawn what kind of writing she did. Shawn happily explained that while she wrote novels, she also wrote magazine articles and some other things occasionally.

"I was just wondering if you might be interested in working on a photography book," Tracy said from the back seat. "I've always wanted to put something together but I don't have the talent for prose. I'm looking for a co-author."

"I'd have to think about that," Shawn said. "It's out of my usual repertoire but we could talk about it."

"Well, how about if I give you one of my cards? If you're interested, you can call me later."

Carrie didn't say anything. It was none of her business if Shawn wanted to work with Tracy. After all, Tracy was a talented photographer and Shawn was a talented writer. This kind of thing probably happened all the time—collaborations, that is, business collaborations.

Tracy had fished out a business card, written something on the back, and handed it to Shawn. Carrie noticed Tracy had lingered a bit while handing it to her, pointing out her cell number written on the back. Well, at least Shawn didn't give Tracy a business card in return.

"Call me," Tracy said to Shawn. "I'd love to talk about it more, if you're at all interested. Maybe we could discuss it over dinner together some time."

"Um, well, I'll think about it," Shawn said, shoving the card into her shorts pocket. She turned to Carrie. "Ready to head home?"

"Sure, any time you are."

Tracy hugged a surprised Carrie. "I'm so glad we met. I hope we'll see more of each other." She went to Shawn and hugged her as well. "And I definitely hope to hear from you, too. Don't lose that card."

Shawn and Kelly gave each other a brief hug. Afterward, Kelly took Carrie's hand once again and kissed the back of her fingers. "And you, fair lady, I'm very happy to see again. I hope to see a lot more of you now that you and Shawn are friends. I hope you'll consider me a friend as well."

"Of course, Kelly. I hope I'll see more of you, too."

Shawn claimed Carrie's hand. "All right, Kelly. That's enough for tonight. See you guys later."

Carrie hoped that meant that Shawn was a little possessive of her, but it could just mean she was ready to go home. At Carrie's place, Shawn walked her up to her door, waiting while she unlocked it. Carrie reached for Shawn's hand. "Would you like to come in for a bit?"

"Sure." Shawn smiled.

They stepped inside and the front door closed. They were still in semi-darkness when Shawn put her arm around Carrie and kissed her. Carrie could feel her insides starting to turn to gelatin as she wrapped her arms around Shawn's neck and deepened the kiss.

Shawn pulled Carrie closer, their breasts touching. Carrie ran her fingers through Shawn's wavy hair, pulling her closer as their tongues danced together. Shawn broke the kiss. Carrie felt Shawn's breathing in her ear, and then her neck, as Shawn trailed small kisses from Carrie's earlobe to her collarbone. Carrie released a small moan, along with Shawn's name, as she leaned into those kisses. She heard Shawn's breathing quicken. She already felt a throbbing and wetness, nearly having an orgasm from just Shawn's kisses. *What would it be like if they made love?*

Carrie felt as if she might explode this time if something else didn't happen. But it was not to be. Shawn backed away and kissed her one more time softly on the lips. She said goodnight, and was gone.

Crap! I don't believe it. Is she playing with me? Once again, Carrie watched the front light come on as Shawn got back into her Jeep and drove into the night. *Damn!* Carrie knew she was going to slip between the sheets naked tonight and ease that ache between her legs herself, just as she had done on several occasions in the past. One of these days, Shawn was not going to run away. One of these nights, she hoped, Shawn would not stop with kisses. *One of these nights… Well, it was not going to be tonight.*

***

Shawn was also ready to slide between the sheets to ease her own ache. She knew Carrie wanted her. She knew she wanted Carrie. She came very close tonight to taking her to bed. *Damn, Carrie feels so good.* She knew in her soul that making love to Carrie would be mind-blowing. But she also knew if she slept with Carrie it would mean more to Carrie than she was ready to give her right now. So she left before it went any further.

Shawn felt bad about leaving Carrie like that, but she didn't know what else to do. She didn't want to lose Carrie—they were already friends and had a great time together. She loved being around her. She loved talking to her. Hell, she loved kissing her. But she just wasn't ready yet for the rest. She didn't know when she would be ready. She wasn't even sure how she'd know if she was ready. *Stupid. This is just awful.*

Well, you keep putting yourself and Carrie into this position. You know you want her. She thought about trailing those kisses farther down onto the swell of Carrie's breast, cupping her breast with her hand and hearing her moan again. Hearing her name. Knowing Carrie wanted her. She almost got back out of bed, put on her clothes, ran down to Carrie's house and banged on the door begging to be let in. But she didn't.

Shawn sighed. She knew she shouldn't be doing this to Carrie or herself. She shouldn't make herself crazy wanting her. She shouldn't be playing the "come here, go away" game with her. Maybe she should stop now with Carrie. Maybe she should try to hook Carrie up with Kelly. They seemed to hit it off. Kelly was also obviously taken with Carrie. Shawn knew the only thing stopping Kelly from asking Carrie out was their friendship. Kelly didn't seem to be involved with Tracy and Tracy definitely didn't seem that attached to Kelly much more than just friends.

But could she stand by and watch someone else kissing Carrie or holding Carrie's hand or putting her arm around her or touching her? Hell, she nearly went crazy when she thought Carrie and Jess had something going on again. Well, that was just wrong. Those two just didn't belong together. Kelly might make Carrie happy. Maybe she should step back and let that situation evolve? She didn't know what she was going to do about this. *Sleep on it, Shawn, old girl. Something will work out tomorrow or the next day.* It had to. She couldn't keep on like this. For Carrie's sake and her own, she had to do something. It just wasn't fair to either of them.

CHAPTER NINETEEN

AS SHAWN SORTED LAUNDRY a few days later, she put her hand in each of the pockets to check them as usual. There was Tracy's card, bent up from being wadded into the laundry. She groaned inwardly and started to toss it in the trash. Something stopped her from letting go of it, so she laid it on the top of the dresser and went on sorting laundry. She had not called or seen Carrie. She knew she was an idiot, but she didn't know what to say to her.

Later, when she picked up Tracy's card again, she noticed something else written on it besides Tracy's cell number. *Call me. I'll make it worth your while.* She toyed with the idea of calling Tracy and finding out more about this photography book she was planning. She wasn't blind. She could tell Tracy was flirting with her. She also knew that Tracy was no romance novel romantic. She was just out to have a good time. As crass as it sounded, even thinking of it, a fun evening in bed with Tracy didn't sound that bad. She and Carrie were not a couple, no commitments of any kind. Heck she didn't even know if Carrie had another girlfriend. It had never occurred to her to ask. If Tracy really was planning a book, it might be fun to work on something different than her usual novels and magazine articles. Shawn picked up the phone and dialed Tracy's cell number.

"Hi, you've reached Creamer Photography," Tracy's recorded voice said brightly. "Please leave your name, phone number, and a brief message. I'll call you back shortly. Thanks!" When the beep sounded, Shawn changed her mind and ended the call.

Well that was stupid, Shawn. Are you going to call her or not? It's a business call. But before she could hit redial, her phone announced an incoming call. The Caller ID said Creamer Photography.

"This is Shawn."

"Well, hi there. I saw your number in my phone as a hang up. Forget what you called about?"

"Uh, no. I had another call come in and figured I'd call you back," Shawn lied.

"Since you didn't leave a message, I thought I'd call you."

There was a brief silence. "Well, I thought about what you said about putting a book together, and it might be fun to work on something like that. I haven't done anything along those lines, but we could talk about it."

"Delightful! Would you like to come to my place for dinner? I could show you what I have in mind, and we could talk about what I would like you to do...Professionally I mean." She laughed.

"Right. Well, that would be all right. When would you like to get together? "

"How about tomorrow night? About eight? I can text you my home address so you can map it, but it's pretty easy to find. I live in the River's Edge development. I'll probably just throw a couple of steaks on the grill, so please just come on over dressed however you're most comfortable.

"That works for me. Can I bring anything?"

"Oh no, you don't need to bring anything but your own sexy self... " Tracy drawled.

"Uh, all right. I'll watch for your text and see you tomorrow night." Shawn hit end on her phone and suddenly felt rather dirty. *That was silly, this is just business. Right. So why do you feel like you're about to cheat on Carrie?*

CHAPTER TWENTY

AT TEN TO EIGHT, Shawn pulled into the River's Edge parking lot. Tracy's condominium was right on the bank of the Caloosahatchee River. This looked like a high rent district, she thought, for a so-called struggling photographer. Come to think of it, though, she never said she was struggling, just that she "paid the bills" by doing portrait photography at the mall. Interesting.

She found Tracy's place easily and pushed the buzzer. Tracy answered the door barefoot and dressed in a very short tropical print sarong tied at her breasts, and nothing else as far as Shawn could tell. If Shawn had been a cartoon character, she knew her eyeballs would've been on springs, leaping out of her head and bouncing around. She had noticed that Tracy had a cute figure the other night, but that sarong really left little to the imagination. Shawn made herself assume there was probably a swimsuit of some kind under there. Even that did little to stop her brain from wandering.

Tracy grinned broadly and reached for Shawn's hand. "Come on in. Don't just stand there. I won't bite." Tracy laughed, a low, throaty sound that did nothing to help Shawn's brain kick back into normal gear. "Let me show you around. My studio is in the downstairs bedroom. Well, it isn't a bedroom anymore."

Shawn could smell steaks cooking somewhere. "Don't you need to check on the steaks? They smell like they need attention."

"Nah, they're fine. I just took them off the grill and put them in the oven to stay warm. We'll eat in a few minutes. I want to show you what you're getting into, so I laid out some things for you to see."

Shawn followed her down a short hall and into a nice sized room with a large worktable. "My darkroom," she motioned toward a door leading to an adjacent bathroom. "It's also a guest bath when people come over."

Tracy had something like a dozen photos laid out on the work table, all appeared to be of local beaches or historical spots on Sanibel and Captiva Islands. She picked up and shuffled through the pictures as she showed them to Shawn. "What do you think?"

"They're very nice. What's the theme of the book? Is it just the islands or do you have more of the Fort Myers area?"

"They're mostly of Sanibel and Captiva. A few shots are of Fort Myers Beach, and I took some out on Pine Island. What ties them all together is the wildlife. Some of the critters I photographed are endangered now, but all of it could be endangered if not preserved. That's the idea behind this book...to show what we have currently and what we could lose if it's not taken care of."

"Very nice idea. Your photographs are not the standard pictures of the beach, so that's great. You've enough passion for this that you should be able to write the prose yourself. I don't think you really need me to do that."

"Oh, I want you, Shawn." Tracy looked straight into Shawn's eyes and ran her hand down Shawn's arm slowly. "I think a real writer could do a much better job. Anyway, enough of this for now. I promised you dinner, and it's ready." She put her arm around Shawn's and led her from the room. Once in the living room, Tracy released Shawn's arm, but trailed her fingers down her hand before letting go. She pointed to the patio. "Right through that door. I'll be out with dinner."

"Can I help?"

"How sweet of you to ask, but I'll be right there. There's some beer in the cooler, several different kinds, so help yourself. Oh, and you can get a Corona out for me."

Out on the back patio, Shawn found a table set up for two with a cooler by the door. She opened two Coronas, placing one on the table and opening one for herself. The view from the patio made these condos so expensive. She could see across the mile-wide Caloosahatchee to the upscale homes on the other side with their boatlifts and party decks. Some had boats the size of yachts moored at docks along the sea wall. Just as she was wondering what one specific boat cost, she heard the slider open and she hurried to help Tracy carry the food out.

"Thanks! I'm so used to doing this myself, but it was nice to have someone help. Especially someone like you."

"Dinner smells and looks delicious. The view is wonderful, too," Shawn turned again to gaze across the river. "I guess you're used to the view, living here. Does it ever get old? Looking at the river I mean."

"No, it doesn't. I love it. What's nice is that the condo association takes care of mowing all the grass and the rest of the outside upkeep, so I can just enjoy the view. We recently had the seawall redone, creating a river walk along it. We can take a stroll out there after dinner if you want. It's really pretty at dusk when the lights along the other side of the river start to come on...It's very romantic."

"I'm sure it is," Shawn's attention came back to Tracy. "I don't know if I'll be here late enough for that, though."

"Oh, you don't have to rush off tonight. You could stick around and enjoy the view for a while." Tracy reached over to brush her fingers across the top of Shawn's hand.

Shawn pulled her hand back, and then reached for her drink. "Well, let's see. Now, about that book of yours..."

"Yes, my...our book," Tracy said, grinning. "Let's talk about that after we finish dinner."

An hour later, and a few more Coronas, and Shawn was feeling rather more relaxed. She also had to pee. Coming out of the downstairs bathroom, she found Tracy waiting in the living room for her. She could see it was starting to get dark outside on the patio, where Tracy had lit a couple of jar candles.

"I'd like to show you something." Tracy said. "There's a special reason I love living here."

"What would that be?"

"Come upstairs with me." Tracy moved toward the staircase. Shawn's eyes followed the line of her thigh exposed by the sarong as she climbed the first stair.

"Why, Mrs. Robinson, are you trying to seduce me?" Shawn laughed.

"Ah, you like old movies?" Tracy laughed, a low, throaty sound. "Maybe I am, but there's something else. Come on." Tracy reached for Shawn's hand and led her up the curving staircase. She led her into what was obviously the master suite, a much larger room with a wall of windows facing the river, directly above the patio. Darkness was falling fast and she could see lights were coming on across the river, dancing on the waves kicked up by the evening breeze. Boats with fore and aft lights slowly drifted either upriver toward Lake Okeechobee or down toward the Gulf of Mexico.

"Wow, what a spectacular view!" Shawn said. "No wonder you like it here. This would be quite nice to wake up to or go to sleep with."

"It definitely is," Tracy said softly. "It is even nicer with someone to go to sleep or wake up with," she whispered, standing closer and running her fingers lightly up Shawn's arm to her shoulder.

Shawn took a deep breath. This was what she had sort of thought and maybe even hoped would happen. But it just didn't feel right. Standing there in the twilight of Tracy's room with the river view spread out below them, it was not as easy to decide what she wanted to do. Or what she should do, for that matter. Tracy was one luscious woman, for sure, and she was very obvious with her intentions. Shawn's insides thought whatever Tracy had in mind sounded like a good idea. Hell, the rest of her body was quickly joining in on that vote.

Tracy reached up and kissed Shawn once, lightly. She didn't wait to see whether Shawn was receptive or not before she kissed her again, and this time Shawn kissed her back. Shawn suddenly felt drawn underwater. She could feel her body responding to Tracy's touch, her kisses. Standing there in the deepening shadows, she was done for.

CHAPTER TWENTY-ONE

CARRIE HADN'T SEEN SHAWN for a few days. Her last view of her had been her back as she walked out of the porch floodlight to her Jeep, leaving her standing there wanting her. Shawn's house was nearly finished, and she hoped to throw her a little housewarming celebration in honor of the new addition.

She wanted to just happen upon her and talk to her about it. She missed seeing Shawn like they used to nearly every afternoon. She looked forward to Shawn being funny or silly or trying to impress her with learning to ride her bike. Of course that was when Shawn had just moved back to the neighborhood.

Carrie finally decided to walk over to see if she was okay. At least that's what she told herself. She brought a note with her that she had written to put on the door if Shawn didn't answer: *Shawn – Haven't seen you for a few days and missed you. Give me a call when you get home? Carrie*

When Carrie got to Shawn's house, the familiar red Jeep was nowhere in sight. Well, she figured, Shawn must be out doing something, so she must be okay. Carrie left the note tucked in the door and walked home.

***

Shawn arrived home the next morning after Tracy made them breakfast. She couldn't believe she'd just spent the night having totally forgettable sex with such a beautiful woman. It wasn't that Tracy didn't turn her on. She did. It must've been good, but in spite of a thorough search of her own brain, she couldn't remember what happened past the first kiss or two. She did remember fantasizing that she was with Carrie when Tracy kissed her.

As she walked up to her front door she saw the note from Carrie.

She sat on the front porch chair and read it. *Damn, she must've put it there yesterday. Now what should I do? I could just...well I should just...* She ran her fingers through her hair and leaned back in the chair, staring at the porch ceiling. *I could just wait till Carrie gets home and call her then. Or should I call her now? No, that would just make it obvious that I just now saw the note. Am I trying to hide what I did last night from Carrie? Yes, that's exactly what I'm doing. I'm overrun with pure unadulterated guilt. Oh God, now what do I do?*

She wanted Carrie, but didn't want to sleep with her unless she felt she could give her that romantic promise that Carrie wanted. She wasn't ready for that yet. She didn't really want Tracy, but she slept with her anyway because she didn't have any problem with what Tracy wanted. Tracy just wanted a good time. Shawn wanted to have a physical release with someone other than her own right hand. If there was nothing wrong with that, then why did she feel awful? She needed to get away and think. She called her publisher.

"Hey AJ. Are you finally ready to take some time off? How would you like to get away from it all for a few days? Are you up for a fishing trip?"

"Well, now, you might be able to talk me into something. I don't know about fishing so much, but how about some chill time out at the cabin in the Smokies? Come to think of it, we might find some fishing up there."

"Sounds good to me. I just need to get away for a while. How soon can we go?"

"Come on up and we can leave in a few days," AJ said. "Meantime, you can zone out at my place. Atlanta's a pretty good place to lose yourself if that's what you want. Do you want to tell me what's going on?"

"Not yet. Not over the phone. How about if I tell you when I get there and we can have a couple of drinks to wash it down?"

"Good plan. See you in a couple?"

"If it's okay, how about tomorrow night?"

"That's fine. I'll stock the bar and the munchies and we'll solve the problems of Shawn's world."

"I'll drive up tomorrow, then. Hey, thanks for being a good friend. I do appreciate you."

"Don't be silly. We've been there for each other for years. You'd do the same for me. Hell, you've done the same for me. Several times. See you tomorrow night."

Shawn smiled as she hit the end button. AJ was right. They'd been through a lot together over the years. AJ had been through several relationships that ended badly, not to mention business setbacks. Shawn had avoided the relationship thing completely until Jen came along. AJ was there to catch her after that one, and had come out to California for a week to listen to Shawn rant, rave, cry, get drunk, and sulk through dealing with her breakup. AJ had also pestered, cajoled, and cheered Shawn through several of her last books. Yes, they'd been there for each other. And they were about to do it again.

Shawn began packing. She hoped she could come to terms with the Carrie situation while she was away. That's what she needed—a clear head. She called Carrie.

"Shawn! Glad you called," Carrie said. "I missed you. I guess you got my note. Well, yeah, of course you did. Sorry I'm rambling. I hadn't seen you for a few days and I was just concerned. Everything okay?"

"Um, yeah...okay. Listen, I need to run up to Atlanta. I'm driving up first thing tomorrow and I'll be gone for a while...taking care of some business with my publisher."

"Oh. Well, would you like to come over tonight for a little while? I made a chocolate pie yesterday."

Shawn started to just say no, then paused. *Chocolate pie. Why did it have to be chocolate pie – one of the few things I can't resist?* "That sounds nice. I'd love to. Want me to give you a call when I'm on my way over?"

"All right. See you this evening."

CHAPTER TWENTY-TWO

CARRIE OPENED THE DOOR just as Shawn reached out to hit the doorbell. "Hi, I saw you coming."

"Hi yourself." Shawn tried to not stare at the undone button on Carrie's blouse, showing a bit more cleavage than usual. She made a point of looking right into Carrie's rich brown eyes, but that just made it worse. She took a deep breath, which she could tell Carrie was mistaking for a yawn. She decided a yawn was a good cover, and pretended a little one, then apologized. "Sorry, been really busy lately."

Carrie invited her to sit at the small kitchen table, where a tiny lit jar candle gave off just a hint of the fragrance of oranges.

"I figured as much when I hadn't seen you for a while," Carrie said. "I used to see you out there pretty much every day, but I haven't seen you running in days. I hoped you didn't get injured or something. Would you like some coffee with your pie?"

"Sure, love some." Shawn sat at the table. "No, I didn't hurt anything. I've just been busy. I need to get back out there running again especially after this pie. It looks wonderful."

"It's my grandmother's recipe. She could whip up a meringue with a fork, of all things. She was a little bitty thing, but we didn't cross her. She was strong. She was a wonderful woman and we loved her very much. You would've liked her...Every time I make that pie I think of her."

"I think it's wonderful that you have something that reminds you of her so much," Shawn said. "You were very lucky you had her, and lucky again to get her pie recipe."

"Believe me, I never forget how fortunate I was to have her around. To get the pie recipe, though, I had to stand right next to her and write down everything she did. She never measured a thing—just a pinch of this and a handful of that. I measured everything she put in it as she made it. It took twice as long, probably. She could practically make pies in her sleep." Carrie placed a piece of the chocolate pie, on a small flowered china plate, in front of Shawn. "Now, this doesn't taste exactly like my grandmother's. We swore that she put her finger in it or something. Finally I decided it had to be just because it was her making it. Things always taste different when someone else makes them."

Shawn took a bite. "Oh, my God!" She took another bite. "Mmm. This stuff is heaven. No wonder you spent all that time with your grandmother learning to make it." She paused for a second or two. "Seriously, this has got to be the best chocolate pie I've ever had. And believe me, I don't say that lightly."

Carrie slowly ate her pie, savoring each bite. She smiled at the compliment. "Thanks. I don't make it unless I'm giving it to someone, bringing it to work, or having company. Otherwise, I'd sit down and eat a whole pie all by myself." She laughed. "And we know that wouldn't be a good idea. I'd have to do an awful lot of bike riding to work that off!"

"I can relate to that. I sure don't want to think about how many miles I'd have to run to do the same thing. I do appreciate you sharing this luscious pie with me. It's wonderful." Shawn took the last bite of her slice of pie, pushed the plate back, and reached for her coffee cup.

"So can I be nosy and ask what you're working on up in Atlanta? A new contract or something?" Carrie also picked up her coffee mug and took a sip.

"Something like that. Actually, my publisher and I are old friends. The last few years while I was in California, we didn't get much time to spend together. So although we'll talk business, we're planning to have some fun too. We may head to the mountains and go camping. We both deserve some time off, now that my book is finally done. She will, of course, start the pressure for the next one." Shawn rolled her eyes. "She never stops being the publisher."

"Good thing you guys are such close friends. I'd bet it must make it easier to get business done, too. You probably don't fight too much about royalties and the like."

"Nah, my guy talks to her guy and they thrash it out. We don't get into that personally very often. We decided a long time ago not to let business interfere with our friendship, and it's worked for quite a while."

"Must be nice to have a friend like that. Growing up, we moved around so much that I never had any friends that lasted very long. I knew I'd be leaving again and would never see them again. So I learned not to get close to anyone. It wasn't till I went to college that I realized that was not a normal way to live. I had the same circle of friends, pretty much, for the four years I was there. After we all graduated and went our separate ways, with our very separate lives, that was pretty much that."

"You didn't try to stay in touch with any of them? Wasn't there anyone special?" Shawn sipped her coffee.

"Well, there was one someone I was quite close to. We were even lovers for a while. But I realized after graduation that she was just 'going through a phase' as they say. You know, girls who want to try stuff just because they can. I think I was her experiment our senior year. She got married a few months later to a lawyer. I saw on Facebook that she's happy raising her kids and being a wife."

"It happens. Sorry about that."

"That was a long time ago. I have friends here, now that I live in one place. Rich and his wife are practically family. Of course there's Jess…" Carrie rolled her eyes as she said it, making them both laugh.

"What about your parents? Do they live here?"

"They used to. Dad had a heart attack and passed away a few years ago. Mom didn't want to stay here anymore and moved up to Memphis to live near her sister. Since I'm an only child, I sort of adopted Rich and his family as my aunt and uncle, along with his kids as my cousins. They adopted me back. It works. They're very nice people. I have to admit I envy you a bit having a friend for so long. Someone who 'knew you when' if you know what I mean."

"I do. Someone who has stories about you as much as you do about them. I'd say that pretty much describes my relationship with AJ…and Kelly too, for that matter."

Carrie picked up the two plates and took them to the sink. She turned and looked at Shawn. "I like being friends with you. I think we could be friends like that."

"I like being friends with you as well." Shawn picked up the two coffee mugs and carried them to the sink. She stood close to Carrie and put her arm around her shoulders. "I like you very much. Plus, you make a great chocolate pie." She laughed. "I'll be your friend forever if you keep plying me with any kind of pie, but especially chocolate."

"Oh, you!" Carrie swatted Shawn with a dish towel. "Here I was being serious."

"So was I. I love pie!"

"Do you have any idea how long you'll be gone? Should I pick up your newspaper or something?" Carrie asked as they walked into the living room.

"Oh, no, that's fine. I called today to tell them to interrupt the News-Press, and I went down to the Post Office already to ask them to hold my mail. I don't expect anything exciting, so it can all wait."

They sat down on the sofa, thighs touching. "I'll miss you while you're gone."

"I'll miss you, too." Shawn reached for Carrie's hand and held it briefly before kissing the back of it. "Very much," she added, looking into Carrie's brown eyes. *Those beautiful eyes with tiny flecks of gold in them. And those long eyelashes. Oh, my God.*

Shawn put her arm around Carrie and drew her closer. Carrie snuggled in, released a little sigh, and cuddled her head into that little spot on Shawn's shoulder where it seemed to fit perfectly.

At the sound of Carrie's sigh, Shawn's heart rate quickened. Surely it was loud enough for Carrie to hear, too. "Carrie, I..."

"Shush." Carrie silenced whatever Shawn was about to say, first with a finger to Shawn's lips, and then with her lips on Shawn's lips. Shawn yielded to those lips as they deepened the kiss, tasting the chocolate from the pie mixed with coffee still on her lips. She could feel Carrie pulling her closer, leaning back on the sofa. In no time, they were lying together on the sofa with Shawn on top.

Shawn could feel every inch of Carrie's soft but firm body beneath her as she continued her kissing exploration of Carrie's neck and then down to the swell of Carrie's breasts that were revealed by the open neckline of her shirt. She realized she was once again over her head, but this time her brain seemed to be turning off and her libido was ramping up. This was what she had dreamed about. This is what she had thought about when Tracy had been seducing her. Carrie was who she wanted. She could feel the ache between her legs. But then, the brain kicked back on again. She wanted Carrie in the worst way, but not now, not like this. She wanted...she wanted... She needed to step back.

She pulled away from Carrie slowly and kissed her softly on the lips. "I can't do this yet. I'm still not ready." She kissed Carrie on her forehead, like one would kiss a child. Shawn and Carrie both sat up and Shawn rubbed her face with her hands. "I'm very attracted to you, but I just can't make love to you right now. I feel that's what you want, and believe me, I'd love to sleep with you, but I just can't yet."

"Don't worry, it's okay." Carrie took both of Shawn's hands in hers. "Hey, I'm sorry, too. I'd love to have you here with me all night, making love into the early hours and sleeping in on Saturday morning. But I don't want you to do something you aren't ready for yet." She put one hand on Shawn's cheek, turning her face to look at her.

"Whatever you need to do, do it. I'll still be here. I want you, I make no bones about that. But I want you as a friend as well. I'm not going anywhere and I'll be right here when you get back."

"Carrie, I…" Shawn felt her throat close up, her stomach clench. "I have to go. I'm sorry I keep doing this to you. I want you in the worst way, but I'm just not ready yet. I'm so sorry. I really need to go."

"I'm sorry you feel that way. I hope you can get whatever is bothering you resolved soon. Maybe we should just be friends until then." She stood up, bringing Shawn to her feet as well.

"Goodnight, Carrie. See you when I get back?"

"Of course." Carrie reached over and placed a soft kiss on Shawn's cheek. "Have a safe trip."

CHAPTER TWENTY-THREE

EARLY THE NEXT MORNING, Shawn packed up her Jeep, locked the house, and hit I-75 North toward Atlanta. She stopped once outside Tampa near Brandon for a quick breakfast and a take-along Coke with extra ice. Since the regular radio kept going in and out, she switched to satellite for the rest of the ride. She needed the noise to help her keep her thoughts from constantly racing back to Carrie.

Carrie. She took a deep breath and shook her head. Carrie's words last night still echoed in her mind. "I'll be here when you get back. I want you." She kept hearing it over and over. Especially the part about being just friends until Shawn could get herself straightened out. She felt like crap for treating Carrie like she had. Knowing Carrie cared for her was an amazing feeling. She heavily kicked her own ass every mile of the way to Atlanta for sleeping with Tracy. She just knew Carrie would never understand why she could do such a thing. Hell, she couldn't understand it herself.

Too bad she couldn't just crawl under a rock and stay there. How she could face Carrie last night and eat that chocolate pie at her house was beyond her. Her head ached. Her stomach churned. She couldn't face Kelly either. She knew Kelly really liked Carrie and would've jumped all over her for what she had done. She needed someone outside the situation. She needed to get away. She needed to think or maybe she thought too much. She had no idea, but she knew she needed to deal with this soon. Talking it out with AJ would be just what she needed. AJ could kick her ass and tell her what to do about this.

She felt overwhelmed with guilt, but like a moth to a flame, she was so drawn to Carrie that she couldn't stay away. It had taken her a year to get over Jen and she was still afraid of making another mistake. She kept shaking her head, thinking maybe an idea would shake loose or the answer would come to her somehow. As the hours and the miles went by, she was only closer to one thing—Atlanta.

***

Carrie noticed Shawn's Jeep was gone by the time she left for work. *Safe trip, Shawn. Whatever it is you have to do, please come back.* She had a feeling Shawn might be going away to try to sort things out, and she hoped fervently that her friend AJ was the person to help her do just that. During the day, she wondered how far along Shawn was in her trip and whether she might call her when she got there. They didn't talk about anything like that, and Shawn probably wasn't used to letting someone know when she arrived somewhere. But Carrie wished she would.

The drive to Atlanta was a long one. Carrie'd made that trip a few times, so she tried picturing in her mind where Shawn might be at any time—maybe stopping for lunch at a certain place or stretching her legs at one of the rest stops. She knew she was fooling herself to think she would hear from her tonight, but she let herself hope she might. Distracted by her thoughts, she didn't notice when Rich seemingly appeared out of nowhere and waved his hand in front of her face. "Earth to Carrie…Earth to Carrie," he called out in a fake computer-sounding voice.

Carrie blushed, mortified she had been caught daydreaming at work. "I'm sorry Rich. Did you need something?" She quickly reshuffled the papers in front of her.

"Not really. I was just walking by and noticed your mind appeared to be off in la-la land. Are you all right? Something bothering you? You aren't sick are you?"

"Oh, no. I'm fine. I guess I just got distracted for a while there. By the way, I noticed the Richards house appears to be about done, at least from the outside."

"Yes, we actually finished a couple of days ago. Shawn signed off on it after the final walk through." He handed her a folder. "Here's her file, ready for the final invoice."

"Nice. I'm sure she's very happy with it."

"She seemed to be. We helped her move her bedroom furniture into the new addition and she now has her living room back and her nice new office that she had wanted. She didn't have stuff for the office yet, but we installed the built-in bookshelves and added a nice window seat as part of her wish list. Practically every wall in that room is covered with bookshelves. She told me she has an extensive library, and now it should all have a nice home. You can send her the final invoice. She said to e-mail it to her."

"She did? Well, that's a good idea, since she said last night that she's going to be out of town for a while."

"Last night? You, uh, saw her last night, did you?" Rich cocked his head to the side and looked at her sideways, giving her a lopsided grin.

"Now, don't you make anything more out of it than it was. I invited her over for dessert last night. We are neighbors, after all."

"Oh really. It wasn't some of your famous chocolate pie, now was it?" He grinned wider at her.

"As a matter of fact, it was. And guess what, there's some for you in the fridge. Like I wouldn't bring you some. Or did you already see it in there?"

"No, I didn't, but I'll head in there shortly and cut myself just a taste with morning coffee. So, you and Shawn have progressed to being friends?"

"Friends. Neighbors. We went out once or twice. That's it."

"You like her, don't you? I can see it in your face. I knew she was just the type you would fall for—tall, good looking, and writes novels. Not to mention just happens to live right down the street. Handy, huh?"

"I do like her. We're becoming good friends. But that's it so far. Just friends."

Rich sat on the side of Carrie's desk. "Hey, I like her too. But I think the world of you. I'm not sure she's who you think she is. I mean, she's nice and all that. Funny as all get out. She joked around with the crew when they were there. But I don't get the impression she's the settling down type of person. You, my dear girl, are the settling down type."

"I am, but I think somewhere inside her is the same type. She might just be the one I've been looking for." Carrie turned around in her chair to face him. "I know you kind of look after me like family, especially after Dad died and I appreciate that. Right now, though, Shawn and I are just friends. That's all."

"Well, I just don't want to see you get your heart broken. You've had a fair amount of unhappiness in the last few years, and I wouldn't want to see more land on you."

"I'm good, really. It's nice having her as a friend. Don't worry."

"Fine, then. I won't worry." Rich stood and took a couple of steps back toward his office, then stopped. He turned around and looked at Carrie, head tilted. "I hope you didn't think I was being too nosey. Karen and I do care about you. I know I'm not your dad or even your uncle, so just tell me to mind my own business if you like."

Carrie grinned at him. "Rich, you know you're the closest thing to family I have around here. But if you do get too nosey, I'll definitely tell you to mind your own business and stick your nose somewhere else." She chuckled. "But you aren't there...yet."

"Good, now, get back to work. Oh, and thanks for the pie."

As Rich's door closed, Carrie shook her head in amusement. She knew how lucky she was to work for someone as great as Rich. And she knew she was lucky again to meet someone like Shawn. She just hoped Shawn got her head straightened out up north, and came back soon.

CHAPTER TWENTY-FOUR

SHAWN PULLED INTO AJ'S driveway as it started to get dark. A huge grin lit up her face as she got out of the Jeep when she saw AJ striding down the front walk.

"Hey, it's my favorite author!" AJ called out and grabbed her in a big hug. She was as tall as Shawn's five foot ten, but where Shawn was lanky, she was more substantial. They looked enough alike to be cousins, at least, with the same sandy hair and blue eyes.

"Hey, it's my nemesis of a publisher who's about to crush me," Shawn said, just before AJ released her.

"Here, let me help you with your stuff. Come on in and let's get caught up." AJ grabbed Shawn's bag out of the back of the Jeep as Shawn carried in her case with her laptop and her fishing gear. They stowed Shawn's things in the guest room and headed to the living room where an open bottle of wine awaited them on a side table.

"What, no JB?" Shawn asked. "You turned into a wine drinker when I wasn't looking?"

"Yeah, I've had to attend quite a few receptions in the last couple of years, and acquired a taste for it. Thought it might be just the thing after a long drive. There's some JB in here if you'd rather have it, though." AJ started to reach into the cabinet.

Shawn put her hand up to stop her. "Nah, a glass of wine is probably just what I need right now," she said, yawning. "It took a couple of hours longer to get here than I'd planned due to that construction again on the interstate around Gainesville and again farther up toward the state line. I guess they try to get this stuff done before tourist season starts. Geez, it's not even that late, but I'm drained."

"This should get you relaxed enough to sleep, then," AJ said, handing her a glass of chardonnay. "We can just enjoy a glass, and then you can head on off to bed if you like. There's a television in your room, in case you want to go to sleep with it on like you used to when you were tired. I'm sure the Science Channel will show a documentary you've seen before that you can listen to and conk out."

"Thanks. I might just do that," Shawn said. "You aren't prodding me with questions, yet?"

"Nope. I just now decided it can wait, even as nosey as I am. I figure I'll do all the prodding tomorrow or up at the camp. Tonight, just relax. Unless you want to tell me something, I won't grill you. I take that back, there's one question: This does have something to do with a woman, doesn't it?"

Shawn wordlessly glanced down at her wine glass, and then looked back up at AJ.

"I kind of figured. No problem, that's all I'll ask tonight."

"Thanks. I knew there was a reason I still liked you." Shawn took a sip of the wine. "Sometimes I just don't know what's good for me. But right now, a nice hot shower and an early bedtime sound pretty damn good."

"Look, we've been friends most of our adult lives, it feels like," AJ examined her wine glass after a sip. "There's nothing much we haven't seen or been through that we couldn't share with each other, when we needed someone to share it with. That means good and bad. The hard stuff and the great stuff."

Shawn nodded. "That is very true, my friend. Very true. I do seem to share more of the hard or bad stuff with you, although you never seem to mind."

"Of course not. Your stuff is always much more interesting than mine." AJ laughed, causing Shawn to smile. "Aw, come on. You know that's true. I'm supposed to be living the glamorous life of a publisher. Like my life is glamorous." She rolled her eyes. "But you seem to wind up with the interesting problems, and they usually involve women. Maybe it's time for you to think about settling down and getting out of the women-problems business."

"Have you forgotten already that I tried that? It's been a year since that ended, but it's still in the back of my mind all the time. I guess I don't want to go through that again."

"Well, that'll be for you to decide, won't it? But not tonight. Tonight you relax and just sleep on it."

"Good idea." Shawn tipped her glass up and drained it. "Nice wine. But maybe tomorrow night or the next we could make some margaritas while you ply me with questions and we solve the problems of Shawn's world. Or we could just have margaritas and solve the rest of the world's problems."

"Deal, but only if you make them. You always could make a killer margarita."

"All right, then. Well, I think I'll turn in right after a nice warm shower and a couple of chapters of reading. Time to hibernate for the evening. Sure you don't mind?"

"Hell no." AJ stood up and stretched. "I've got at least all next week to spend with you, so one evening isn't a big deal. Besides, if I'd driven all day, all I'd want to do is what you do: crash. If you want anything, you know where the kitchen is. Help yourself. I think I'll go hibernate as well. It's been a busy week. Oh, by the way, there's some rocky road ice cream in the freezer. I just thought you might need it."

"You remembered. Another reason I like you. Thanks." Shawn stood up and put her arm around her friend's shoulders. "I love you, you know." Then they finished in unison, "But not like that!" They both laughed and said goodnight as Shawn headed down the hall to her bedroom.

As Shawn pulled the door shut, and began unpacking her overnight stuff, she wondered what Carrie was doing. Before she knew it, she was punching in Carrie's number.

"Hi, there. Did you get there in one piece?" Carrie asked.

"I'm fine. I was just thinking about you, that's all. I thought I'd call and see how the rest of the chocolate pie is doing," Shawn said.

"It's almost gone, as a matter of fact. I took some in to work...Shawn I'm so glad you called. I miss you already. It feels funny for you not to be here. I hope you have a great time up there with your friend, though. You probably need a vacation after finishing your book."

"I do. I miss you, too. Do you think maybe there could be another chocolate pie when I get back?"

"You got it. Just let me know when you're on your way, and it'll be here for you."

Was that a hint of excitement in Carrie's voice? "I'll be looking forward to it. But right now I'm really tired, so I think I'll say goodnight. It's not that late, but all that driving..."

"I get that. I've done that drive and it's a long day. Well, take care of yourself. And I hope you have a great time and the weather holds up for you there."

"Thanks. I'll see you when I get back," Shawn said. "Goodnight."

"Goodnight. Sleep well."

Shawn hung up, almost unwilling to give up the sound of Carrie's voice. She tossed the phone on the nightstand and finished unpacking what she needed. She headed for the shower and turned it on to warm up. As she stripped off her clothes, she realized she did miss Carrie already. She had said it, she thought, just to be nice. But it was true she actually did miss her.

This time last night she had been sitting in Carrie's kitchen eating pie, and then making out on Carrie's sofa like a couple of teenagers. It was more than that, though. She wanted to touch Carrie's skin. She wanted to feel her body and smell her fragrance, like something very clean. She wanted to kiss her. She wanted to make love to her in the worst way. No, scratch that. She wanted to make love to her in the best way. She wanted to make slow, sweet love to her. She was really going to need a shower now, for sure. *Oh no, I'm falling in love with her! But it's too soon. Is a year long enough to grieve over a bad relationship? Is a few months long enough to know whether you're really in love with someone?*

Shawn stepped into the shower and leaned against the shower wall, letting the warm water pelt her skin. She was tired enough to doze off standing there and almost did, it felt so good. But her brain was on overload again, streaking in so many directions that she could feel it ache.

CHAPTER TWENTY-FIVE

THE NEXT DAY CARRIE was waiting at the Smokin' Pit's pickup area for her order, when she heard someone call her name. She realized right away who it was, and decided to pretend she didn't hear. But when Tracy called her name again, she turned around and waved halfheartedly at her. Tracy and Kelly were seated a few booths away by the front window, eating lunch. They waved her over.

"Come, sit with us," Tracy said.

"Oh, no thanks. I'm just here for takeout. It'll be ready in just a minute. I can't stay..." Carrie began.

"You can wait here as well as over there. You can hear them call you from over here." Tracy slid over and patted the bench next to her.

Kelly chimed in, "Come on, sit down for a minute. What've you been up to?"

"Nothing much, just working, as usual," Carrie answered as she slid in next to Tracy. But not too close.

"You and Shawn doing anything this weekend?" Kelly asked.

"No. Didn't she tell you? She's out of town. Went to Atlanta to see her friend AJ. She said something about being gone for a little while."

"Well, honey, we'll have to all do something together then. Right, Kelly?" Tracy said, her voice all maple syrup sugary.

For some reason, Carrie already wanted to throttle her. *What did Kelly see in her? Seriously, is that for real?* She wanted to gag. "I, uh...don't know. Maybe. I don't want to be the third wheel." Carrie looked around toward the takeout desk. "I think I heard them call my name. I'd better go."

"Carrie, you'd never be a third wheel. I'd love to have you come along with whatever we're doing. Tracy and I, well, we're not doing anything much. If you'll give me your number, I'll call you tomorrow. We're thinking about a cookout at my house."

"That sounds like fun," Carrie said as Kelly handed her phone over.

Carrie punched in her number, then handed it back. "Oh, by the way, Shawn called last night. She got to Atlanta in one piece. I guess she just needs a vacation."

"Thanks. I know I'd need one if I'd just finished writing a book. A little R and R is just the thing, I'm sure."

Carrie slid out of the booth and stood up. "I'm sure it is. I'd better go. Talk to you tomorrow."

As Carrie walked back to the pickup area, she overheard Kelly telling Tracy, "See, I told you there was something going on between them." What Tracy said in reply, she couldn't hear, but she hoped that was enough for Tracy to lay off any plans she had for Shawn. *At least Shawn is out of town and well out of Tracy's clutches.*

Carrie picked up her carryout pork ribs and hushpuppies, and headed for her car. *Kelly is such a nice person, how could she stand being around Tracy as a friend, let alone a lover? Oh, no, where did that come from? Tracy has done nothing to me, except to ask politely if Shawn and I were a couple before she said she wanted to ask Shawn out. At least she asked. Maybe I'm being too harsh with Tracy. Just because I find her personally annoying doesn't mean she's not a nice person. Kelly likes her, so she can't be all that bad.*

Okay, maybe I'll try harder to be friends with Tracy. After all, I really like Kelly and Kelly is one of Shawn's best friends, and Kelly likes Tracy. So there we go. When Kelly calls tomorrow, I'll be sure to be friendlier than I was today. I'll try harder to be nice to Tracy, too. Tomorrow.

CHAPTER TWENTY-SIX

CARRIE WAS WORKING AWAY at her desk when Kelly called her cell the next morning.

"Hey Carrie. Hope I'm not interrupting your work, but I wanted to make sure you understood my invitation is for tonight. I'm doing the grilling, but if you want to bring some dessert, that'd be great. Tell me you'll come."

"Of course. I'm looking forward to it. And I'm happy to bring dessert. How about if I bring the makings for sundaes. Does that work?"

"That works very well and sounds like fun. How about six thirty? Do you remember how to get here? If not, I can text you the address and you can map it. Or you can call me if you get lost," Kelly said.

"Go ahead and text me the address just in case, but I'm pretty sure I can find it again. See you at six thirty then."

"Great! I'm looking forward to a sundae for dessert. See ya."

Carrie smiled. She didn't know where she came up with the idea for sundaes but now it sounded quite yummy to her as well. All she needed to do after work then was to run by Publix to pick up the ice cream and toppings. She found herself looking forward to seeing Kelly again. *And Tracy.* She reminded herself she was going to be nice to Tracy.

***

Carrie had no trouble finding Kelly's house again. Once she got into the general vicinity, she remembered where she was going from the last time she was there, with Shawn. She smiled and felt a little glow inside, remembering her conversation with Shawn the other night. It felt nice that Shawn cared enough to call her. In fact, it felt very nice.

As she pulled in, she noticed three vehicles in the driveway. Maybe someone else was coming as well. She thought for a second and determined she brought plenty of ice cream. There would be more than enough for even five or six people.

By the time she reached the door, Kelly was already there, grinning, holding the door open for her. She reached for the cooler bag Carrie brought with her holding the ice cream and the rest of the sundae fixings, and then gave Carrie a quick hug.

"Thanks for coming," Kelly said as they walked toward the kitchen. "Everyone is out back. By the way, Tracy invited a friend to come along, so there are four of us. Don't worry, she's not supposed to be your date. She's actually Tracy's date."

Carrie raised her eyebrows as she looked at Kelly. "I thought you and Tracy..."

"Off and on. Mostly off. We're pretty much just friends. I don't have any problem with her bringing a date. Hey, you can sort of be my date tonight. How's that?"

"Well, since this appears to be a foursome now, I'm good with that. As long as I don't have to adopt you permanently or anything." Carrie laughed. "I don't think I could afford to feed you."

"Oh, now, that's unfair. I don't eat that much!" Kelly said, grinning widely. "Let's get this stuff into the freezer and head out back. I'll introduce you to Tracy's friend."

A few minutes later Carrie stepped outside onto Kelly's patio to see Tracy and a woman who could've been the negative of a picture of Shawn. She was tall and dark, with a nice athletic-looking body that wore clothes well. She and Tracy were locked into a very passionate looking kiss. Kelly stepped out behind Carrie and she cleared her throat dramatically.

"Hey, you two. Enough of that for a while," Kelly said. "Carrie, the person who was just lip-locked with Tracy is Chris."

Chris reached out to shake hands. As Carrie shook her hand, she noticed Chris had some interesting callouses. "So what do you do, Chris?"

"She's a sculptor," Tracy broke in. "She's going to do me." Chris actually blushed. "I mean, she's going to do a figure of me. Geez, you guys."

"Well, you walked right into that one," Kelly said, chuckling. "You're good at that."

"Very funny."

Chris pulled a chair out for Tracy to sit. "Actually I saw her out on Fort Myers Beach. I just walked up and asked her if I could sculpt her.

She thought I was just feeding her a line and I had to prove to her that I really am an artist. Over lunch, I showed her pictures of some of the things I've done, and eventually got her to come to my studio. The rest is history. We just clicked."

"How romantic." Carrie wanted to gag. "So when will we all get to see this piece?"

"Oh, it's not started yet," Tracy said. "She'll start work on it right after she gets finished with her current project. Meantime, we're enjoying each other's company, aren't we sweetie?"

"Oh, yeah." Chris patted Tracy on her bare thigh.

Carrie looked at Kelly, who didn't seem to mind what was going on between Chris and Tracy. This seemed quite odd to Carrie, since she had just been on a double date with them—Kelly and Tracy, that is—a short time ago, and they had been holding hands and acting like they were a couple.

Kelly got up to check on the grilled steaks. Tracy brought some potato salad, and Kelly had also made some grilled vegetables. It was a pleasant dinner, and they all chatted away as they sun began to go down. They brought out the ice cream and toppings and had a great time deciding which toppings to put on which ice cream, along with sprinkles, cherries, nuts, and whipped cream.

"I haven't had anything like this in ages," Kelly said. "Carrie, the sundaes were a great idea. Thanks for thinking of it." She waved her hand across the table, just barely tapping the uncapped chocolate sauce. It fell straight into Carrie's lap. Before she could grab it, a fair amount of sauce was already dripping out onto Carrie's shorts and her leg.

Kelly grabbed the jar and began apologizing as Carrie began dabbing at the chocolate sauce with a napkin. Tracy jumped up. "Come on Carrie – let's find something to get that out before it stains." Carrie stood up and Tracy grabbed her by the arm and led her into the house.

As they looked in the laundry room for some spray stuff to get the chocolate sauce out, Carrie decided it was time to try to make nice with Tracy. "So did you really meet Chris like that on the beach?"

"Pretty much. I was very flattered, of course. But I kind of figured she was coming up with a big line. I mean, really, doesn't it sound like, 'hey baby, let me put you in the movies' or something equally dumb? But she really is a sculptor."

They found the spray stain remover and a cloth and Carrie began working on getting the chocolate out of her shorts.

"So, Carrie, you said yesterday Shawn took off up north for a while?"

"Yes, she left a couple of days ago. Off to see her publisher, she said." Carrie continued to spray and dab.

"I wonder if they're going to talk about my book," Tracy said, leaning her back against the counter.

"Not to sound weird, but why would they be talking about your book?" Carrie looked up at Tracy.

"Well, she came to my place one night and we did discuss working together on my photography book," she paused, then did one of those long slow smiles that everyone knows means something else is coming. "Among other things."

Carrie continued to dab, barely looking up. "Oh, really. She didn't mention it when I saw her the night before she left. But that's business. Maybe she does need to discuss it with her publisher." She finally got most of the chocolate sauce out of her shorts and now she was looking at a huge wet spot. She thought absently that it was a good thing those were not her good white shorts.

"Could be. But we didn't end up talking about the book much when she was over, if you know what I mean," she said, winking at Carrie. "I figured we'd talk some more about it later, but I haven't heard from her since then. When did she leave?"

"Two days ago. Why?"

"Just wondering. She was at my place three nights ago. Oh well, maybe she wasn't that interested in working with me after all. I might not be ready to do it any time soon, anyway. I might be kind of busy for a while. Collaborating with my sculptor friend, if you get what I mean." She laughed.

"Yes, I do. So were you and Shawn collaborating the other night, too?" Carrie held her fingers in the air like quotation marks around collaborating.

"Well, yeah. You said you weren't a couple, so I figured you didn't mind. It was just one night. She got pretty wasted, but it was fun until she passed out."

Carrie felt her stomach grab. She wanted to run. She wanted to pretend she hadn't heard what she just heard. But it was too late. She tried to tell herself that it didn't matter. But it did. Shawn had just told her the night before she left that she couldn't sleep with her yet, that she wasn't ready. Yet, she didn't think twice about jumping into bed with Tracy. She blurted out, "Hey, I've got to go."

"I'm sorry, did I say something?"

"No, Tracy, you didn't." Carrie gave her a little smile. She didn't want to give Tracy the satisfaction of seeing her acting upset. "I'm good. I just can't get all of this chocolate out of my shorts and I need to get them into the wash before they're totally trashed. I'd better go say goodbye to Kelly and Chris."

Carrie found Kelly had finished mopping up the spilled sauce and was sitting at the table once more. She got up when she saw Carrie with that large wet spot on her shorts leg. She pulled out Carrie's chair.

"Oh my God, I'm so sorry, Carrie. You probably think I'm such a klutz. I'm not, normally. Come sit down, and I'll get you some more tea."

"I really can't. I need to get going. My shorts are going to have a permanent chocolate mark on them otherwise." Carrie tugged at the wet leg of her shorts.

Kelly looked at Tracy, who just rolled her eyes and shrugged. Tracy sat back down next to Chris. Kelly followed Carrie back into the house as Carrie picked up her bag.

"Let me get the rest of the ice cream and—" Kelly headed for the kitchen.

"Oh, no. You keep it. I'm sure you can find a use for it." Carrie tried to find a small smile. It wasn't Kelly's fault that she felt like crawling under a bush.

"Well, thanks. I'm sure it'll get eaten. Let me walk you out to your car."

Carrie was silent as they walked out the front door. She beeped her car unlocked and reached for the door handle. Kelly's hand was on hers before she could pull it open.

"What happened in the house, Carrie? You were fine, but when you came back outside you looked like you had been kicked in the stomach."

Carrie turned around slowly and leaned her back against her car. "Are you sure you want to hear this?"

"I'm very sure. I want to know about anything that's bothering you," Kelly said. "I like you a lot and I don't like seeing you hurt. Did Tracy say or do something?"

Carrie wrapped her arms around herself and examined her sandals for a minute. She looked back up at Kelly. "Shawn slept with Tracy," she said softly. Carrie's throat constricted and her stomach felt like a pretzel. She was trying very hard to not sound like some stupid little girl who found out her sweetheart had kissed her best friend.

"Oh," Kelly muttered. She looked away then back at Carrie. "Are you sure? I mean, Tracy can stretch things to suit herself. Maybe they didn't really, and she wanted to brag a little to you anyway."

"I didn't get that feeling. She wasn't even bragging. She just said it matter of factly in conversation, like it was nothing." Carrie brushed away one escapee tear.

"Carrie, I don't mean to pry, but have you and Shawn been together?"

"No, but not because I didn't want to. It is always her who backs away, not me." Carrie examined her feet again. "I thought she just wasn't ready. That's what she said. Is there something wrong with me? I'm not some little goody-two-shoes, as my grandmother used to say. I really care about Shawn. I think she feels something for me as well, and then she did this. Why would she do that?"

"Tracy can have quite an effect, that's for sure. But I'm guessing there was something else involved. I don't know what that something is, but I can't imagine Shawn would intentionally do something to cause you pain. Look, I can tell you're feeling very hurt and probably a bit angry right now. The Shawn I know is not the bed-jumping kind of woman, at least not anymore." Kelly put her arm around Carrie and held her close. "Why don't you come to lunch with me tomorrow and meantime I'll try to get some more information out of Tracy. Maybe I can find out what really happened. Think about it. Call me tomorrow and let me know if you want to get together and talk."

Carrie nodded. She was blinking hard to hold back the tears. "Okay. You know Tracy better than I do, obviously. I thought I had a good bead on Shawn, but maybe I didn't." She shook her head. "Now, I don't know. I just don't know."

"Yeah, I can imagine. Look, I'm under the definite impression that Shawn really likes you. A lot. From the things she's said, I can't imagine that she doesn't. I can't tell you what to feel, but for right now, don't write her off."

"Thanks, Kelly. I'll try hard not to let my imagination run away with me. She did call me from Georgia the evening she got there. She said she missed me. I guess that's something, isn't it?"

"I'd say so. She didn't call me to tell me she missed me." Kelly laughed. Carrie couldn't help smiling. "See, better already. Looks like you'd better get home and get that chocolate out of those shorts," she told Carrie. "I don't want to have to buy you some more, since it was my bumbling that caused the accident."

"You're sweet," Carrie said, looking up into Kelly's eyes. "I never noticed you had green eyes before. They're very pretty."

"Uh, thanks. I can't take credit for them, of course. I, uh, guess I'll see you tomorrow, maybe?"

Carrie nodded.

"Drive home safely then," Kelly said, giving Carrie a little hug. Carrie turned around fully, put her arms around Kelly, and kissed her on the cheek.

"Thanks for being my friend, too. I'll talk to you tomorrow."

Kelly released Carrie, watched as she got into her car, and pulled out of the driveway. As Carrie drove away, Kelly touched the place on her cheek where Carrie had just kissed her. She could still smell Carrie's scent. *Shawn, you might've blown it here, buddy. Should I try to help you, or not?* She took a deep breath as she turned and walked slowly back into her house to rejoin her company.

CHAPTER TWENTY-SEVEN

CARRIE REALIZED SHE'D BEEN sitting in her car in her driveway for a while. She wasn't crying. She didn't even feel mad any more. She finally got out and trudged to the house. Opening the screened porch door, she found a little bouquet of flowers in a vase. Her hands shaking, she picked them up and carried them into the house, placing them on the kitchen table. The tiny card attached to them read: *I really do miss you. Shawn*

Carrie was torn between wanting to cry from being happy and wanting to shred the card and throw the flowers out the back door as far as she could pitch them. She wanted to be angry. Shawn, though, would have no idea that she knew about Tracy—if there was, in fact, something to know. She so hoped Tracy had embellished the story and nothing actually happened. It was possible. She left the flowers on the kitchen table and placed the card next to them.

Once in her room, she mechanically stripped off her stained shorts and the rest of her clothes, wondering what she'd find out from Kelly the next day. Throwing on a long T-shirt, she took the shorts to the utility room and sprayed them again with stain remover, tossed them into the wash, and hit the start button. She stood there and stared at the washer for a minute before she realized what she was doing.

Back in the kitchen, she put on the kettle and waited for the water to heat for the Earl Grey tea that always made her feel better. As she sat at the kitchen table waiting for the whistle on the kettle, she looked at the card again. It still said I really do miss you. She didn't know quite what to make of it. Had she not had Tracy's little revelation this evening, she'd have been very pleased to sit there and look at them. It would've been a sweet end to the day. The vase shaped similar to a little Mason jar held what looked like a bunch of wild flowers, like someone had picked them in a field and brought them to her. She loved them.

The little bird on the kettle whistled that the tea water was ready. Standing at the stove, she looked back at the kitchen table and imagined Shawn still sitting there from three nights ago. It seemed so natural for her to be there. So comfortable to be together. She smiled at the thought, even as a single tear formed in her left eye and then overflowed onto her cheek.

Swiping away the tear with her palm, she sat back down at the table with her mug of Earl Grey and sighed. She looked across the table at the imaginary Shawn and asked, "What am I going to do about you, Shawn Richards? Where do we go from here?" She shook her head. Imaginary Shawn didn't answer.

***

Carrie waited until nearly lunchtime before calling Kelly. She wasn't sure she wanted to know what, if anything, Kelly found out from Tracy. When Kelly answered the phone, though, Carrie didn't want to wait any longer to ask the big question. As soon as Kelly said hello, Carrie asked her, "Do I want to know what happened or not?"

"You do. Do you want the sordid details over the phone or in person?" Kelly started to laugh.

"All right, what's so funny? This situation isn't all that funny to me."

"I'm sorry, Carrie. I promise that when I give you the whole story, you'll think it's funny, too. I swear you will. So, how do you want it?"

"All right, I'll make lunch for us. You can come over here and tell me the whole sordid tale. How's that? Since you think it's funny, I think I'd rather hear it in person. I'm two doors down from Shawn on the same side of the street. I'll text you my address, just to be sure. See you in about half an hour?"

"I'll be there. Do you want me to bring anything? I just happen to have some ice cream and sundae toppings here."

"Well, I just happen to have some pie here. If you want to bring some ice cream to go with it, that'd be just fine. See you in a bit." Carrie texted her address to Kelly as soon as they hung up.

Half an hour later, Kelly was sitting at Carrie's kitchen table enjoying ham sandwiches, potato salad, and sweet tea. Kelly nodded at the little jar of flowers on the table. "Those are pretty."

"From Shawn," Carrie replied, smiling.

"Well, well. What do you know...maybe you're making some progress with that thick-headed idiot. Speaking of," Kelly paused, taking a bite of her sandwich. "Are you ready for the real story about what happened at Tracy's?"

"Let's hear it. How detailed did she get?"

"Pretty detailed. By the way, great sandwich. Love sourdough bread. Anyway, back to the story. First off, Tracy actually had invited her over to talk about collaborating on her photography book. So they honestly were meeting to talk business and did for a little bit. Tracy said she thought she'd have a little fun if Shawn was interested. She kept the alcohol flowing, thinking Shawn might be a little too tipsy to drive home and would stay the night with her, and see what happened. But that's typical Tracy, she just wants to have a good time. She doesn't usually want to keep what she catches."

Carrie was getting a different picture in her mind now of what might've happened. "Go on," she urged Kelly. "I think I can see where this is headed."

Kelly took another bite of her sandwich. "Okay, well, apparently she got Shawn up to her room to 'see the view'. Hey, it worked on me. Anyway, they looked at the view, and Tracy kissed Shawn. She said Shawn did kiss her back, but it was clear Shawn had a bit too much to drink. By the time Tracy got her on the bed, Shawn flat passed out." Kelly laughed some more. "Shawn was obviously not going home, nor was she going to make any mad, passionate love to Tracy. So, Tracy only took advantage of her enough to strip her clothes off her and put her to bed." Kelly paused, watching while Carrie wiped a tear from her eye, but from laughing, not crying. Kelly took another bite of ham, pausing for effect.

"Come on, now, there's more, of course. Give." Carrie leaned forward.

"Here's the good part." Kelly leaned closer as well and lowered her voice conspiratorially. "Tracy got naked, just crawled into bed with her and slept curled up with her all night."

"Wow...really?"

"Really. And there's still more. Now, the next morning, Shawn woke up with Tracy snuggled up to her, nude like I said, and probably assumed what happened...but didn't. Tracy didn't tell her otherwise. She let her think she was the big stud, and all that. She made breakfast for them the next morning, although she said Shawn didn't eat much. She said she figured Shawn had a hangover. And that was it. Shawn left. Just said goodbye and thanked her for a nice evening and breakfast. She didn't kiss her goodbye or say she would call her or anything. Tracy said Shawn looked like she didn't feel very well, though."

"Well, that explains something."

"Explains what?"

"Last night Tracy did say that Shawn was a lot of fun till she passed out," Carrie said, and began giggling. "Now, I haven't seen her drunk, although we've downed a pitcher of margaritas together. Maybe I should've gotten her a little tipsy. That might've done the trick."

"Oh, no. I don't think so." Kelly stopped laughing and looked at Carrie. "Now, here we are having a good laugh at poor Shawn's expense. She's off in Georgia thinking she got drunk and slept with Tracy. She really likes you, but hasn't slept with you."

"So?"

"So I'm betting she's feeling guilty as hell and doesn't know how to deal with it. I know she likes you a lot. I think she really wants to be with you. You're sweet, very pretty, and fun to be with. Besides, there's a light on behind those gorgeous eyes." Kelly lowered her voice. "If I didn't think there was something between you two, I would've asked you out myself. You really are special."

"Oh, Kelly, you're pretty special yourself," Carrie said, reaching to touch Kelly's hand. "You're outstanding at rescuing damsels in distress."

"Damsels in distress?"

"Sorry. Shawn once said you were very good at rescuing damsels in distress. Kind of a knight in shining armor thing. She meant it in the nicest way possible. She admires you, you know. You said that whole Tracy and Shawn thing didn't bother you any more than the Tracy and Chris thing last night, but still..."

"Oh, that was mostly Tracy. Besides, Tracy does what Tracy does. I could never be serious about her or anyone like her. I like her and I consider her a friend. But that's pretty much it. I'm looking for someone...well...someone sort of like you to eventually settle down with one of these days. I'll find her. I just have to keep looking."

"Kelly, you're wonderful. One of these days someone just as wonderful will show up in your life and you'll live happily ever after. And yes, I do read romance novels, but I truly believe there is a happy ever after for everyone. We just have to watch for it and believe it can happen. And you, my knight in shining armor, are just holding out for the right damsel, in distress or not."

"I guess I'll see, huh? Okay, now that we've solved part of your problem, what'll you do about the rest of it now?"

"Nothing much to do until she comes back. She did send me those pretty flowers and she called me once from Georgia. That means something. I'm hoping that it means she wants to resolve her issues. Meantime, there's nothing to do but wait."

CHAPTER TWENTY-EIGHT

"ALL RIGHT…" SHAWN LEANED back in the quad chair and stretched her legs to put her hiking boots up on a stump. "This is the life. Don't have to do anything at all unless we want to. No deadlines, no…signal." She poked at her smart phone as if that would make it connect.

"Well, you said you wanted to get away. We're away," AJ said, handing her a Corona. "The only signal you can get out here might be if you had one of those satellite things. You know, the ones you could make a connection with in the middle of the Sahara."

"Guess I've forgotten what it's like. It does feel a bit strange, though." Shawn shrugged as she put her phone back in the pocket of her shorts.

"If you get too strung out, we can probably get a tower near that town we passed on the way up. We'll have to go there anyway in a day or two for some more ice, if nothing else. No warm beer or soda for me, please."

"Me neither. Still, it's pretty and so nice and quiet back here in the mountains." Shawn picked up a stick and tossed it into the fire, watching the sparks rise with the smoke into the deepening twilight.

"That's why I keep this place, even though there's no power. Keeps it rustic. Speaking of rustic, how's that little cracker house of yours coming along? I couldn't imagine you were actually going to live in that tiny place. It's pretty old, too. It's fine for a getaway, but really, to live in?"

"I know, not your style, but I love that old place. It just suits me. It was around before my parents were born. More like when my grandparents were kids. It reminded me of a place my great-grandparents had. Theirs had been added onto several times, but the bones were the same as this one."

AJ looked at her quizzically.

"You know, classic cracker…straight shot from the front door to the back, so the breeze comes through. Deep screened-in porch. The steeply pitched metal roof. God, I love the sound of rain on a metal roof."

"The way you describe it, it sounds almost romantic. But then again, that's what we pay you for, don't we. So what in the world made you decide to remodel during hurricane season? Wasn't the contractor worried about that?"

"Nah, he was game. He said if he only did construction work in the winter he'd be out of business. Besides, most of the time nothing happens. If it does, well, there's insurance for that, and we fix whatever gets messed up. They know what they're doing, though, and can close up a building tightly if they need to for a storm to pass."

"Um...Shawn?"

"What?"

"Don't move."

"What do you mean, don't move? I hate it when you do that. What is it?" Shawn looked all around trying so see what AJ was looking at.

AJ, meanwhile, reached for a stick from the kindling pile and was aiming it right at Shawn's head like she was going to beat her with it in slow motion. Shawn watched as she moved closer and closer.

"What the hell are you doing?" Shawn stared at AJ like she had just sprouted an extra head.

"Don't. Move. I said."

Shawn did as she was commanded, and suddenly felt the stick swipe hard through her hair. Out of the corner of her eye she could see something go flying. Something dark. Something with legs. She shot up out of her chair, the beer in her hand went flying, and her hands went instantly to her hair, brushing furiously at it. "What the hell was that...please don't tell me it was a spider. Please don't..."

"It was a spider. A big one." AJ threw the stick back into the kindling pile and started snickering. "Oh my God, you're such a girl about spiders. You always have been, though. I figured I'd better get it off of you before you touched it with your hands. You'd have really freaked then. How you can enjoy camping so much but be so afraid of spiders is beyond me."

"Hey, I'm not afraid of them. They just gross me out and I don't want one to touch me. That's all." Shawn paced back and forth running her fingers through her hair over and over. "So much for relaxing and peaceful."

"Oh, come on, sit back down. That thing just happened to fall on you out of the trees. It's gone. Besides, I'm dying to hear you spill about what got you so wound up you needed to get out of Dodge in a hurry. I'm sure this is going to be good." AJ rubbed her hands together like she was going to start a fire with two sticks. "I brought marshmallows...the big ones. While you talk we can roast 'em. How's that?"

Shawn stopped pacing and sighed. This was what she came here for, the patented AJ Intervention. "All right." Shawn picked up the bottle she'd thrown, tossed it into the recycling bag, and sat down hard on the chair. Once her feet were back up on the stump, AJ handed her another drink. Shawn spoke slowly, "It's what you're probably suspecting."

"Oh, no, you aren't still strung out on that whole Jen thing are you?" AJ handed the bag of marshmallows over along with a peeled stick.

"Yes and no. That whole Jen thing as you put it, did make me much more cautious about getting involved with someone else." Shawn pulled out two marshmallows, threaded them onto the stick so they touched, and handed the bag back.

"And...now there's someone else in the picture?" AJ prodded her.

"Yeah. There is."

"So what's the problem, then?"

"She's a very nice someone else. She's pretty. She's sweet. She's smart...she even likes me." Shawn grinned absently, holding her marshmallows toward the fire.

"She does? Wow, what a thought. Still not seeing a problem." AJ laughed.

Shawn backhanded AJ's shoulder with her free hand. "Smartass, be serious."

"All right then, tell me about her and explain why you're already in some kind of trouble. And make it good. I haven't had a good Shawn story in ages. You haven't been much fun for a long time now."

Shawn stared into the fire, turning her marshmallow stick slowly. "I know, but hey, I thought Jen was 'The One.' Boy, was I wrong about that."

"Buddy, you've got to learn to think with something besides your crotch. Jen went after you because of who she thought you were. Everyone saw that but you. She played up to you and you went for it...hook, line, and sinker. She never really knew the real you, and didn't care to. Unfortunately, you catered to that. You hide from almost everyone behind that author persona you've cultivated."

"I know, I know. It's been easy to be that person. She has fun. She can't be hurt because she doesn't let herself care too much. Yeah, I know I'm referring to myself in the third person. But that's what she feels like, another person. I let Jen in somewhat, and I cared. I did. I thought she loved me, but she didn't. The pain when it ended was awful."

"But you didn't die, did you? You learned something from the experience and now you move on, right?" AJ shook her head slowly, smiling. "You're such a big mush bag inside. Sooner or later, you'll let the right woman see that part of you, and she'll love you for it."

Shawn pulled her golden-colored marshmallows from the fire just before they started to scorch. She pulled off the crispy outside layer, stuffed it into her mouth, and then reached the stick with the mushy marshmallow goo still clinging to it back toward the fire for another round. She knew AJ was eager to hear the rest of this story, and as she watched the rest of the marshmallow start to brown, she began.

"Her name is Carrie."

"Carrie...nice name. Tell me more."

"Yeah, Carrie," She exhaled a wistful sigh, "With golden brown hair, pretty, deep brown eyes and a body to make you sweat. She's fun. She's sexy as all get out in a very wholesome way. Athletic type—rides a bike every afternoon—but has curves in all the right places. She looks like some kind of competitive rider with that bike of hers. "

"Really. So how did you meet this nearly perfect woman?"

"Oddly enough, she lives right down the street. We're neighbors."

"What? That's pretty handy. How come you didn't already know her? Did she move there after you went to California?"

"Yes she did, and no it isn't. Think about this...we get involved, we have a breakup in six months or a year, and there she is, still living down the street from me. That could be quite uncomfortable for both of us." Shawn pulled the last of the marshmallow off the stick, shoved it into her mouth, and licked her fingers slowly.

"What makes you think that will happen? How far has this gone so far?"

"Mostly just kissing. She wants more. I want more. We've had a few dates, and hung out at her house or mine just talking."

"Oh, how awful! How can you stand it?" AJ said, grinning.

"Oh, yeah, so hard," Shawn said, not grinning. "She's made it clear she's ready for this relationship to move forward." She paused. "And I want her in the worst way."

"So, what's the issue? Are you thinking she'll be like Jen and dump you when she finds someone else who entertains her more?"

"Kind of. Plus, get this, Carrie is a fan. She's read all my books. She wants her life to be like one of my romance novels, with love on the beach and all that."

"So?"

"So? So?" Shawn threw up her hands, jumped up, and started pacing near the fire. "I'd have to live up to one of my fictional characters. She has this vision of what it should all be like. What if I can't deliver that?"

"Geez, Shawn. If anyone could give her that it'd be you. You wrote the damn things. You must've come up with that stuff from somewhere inside you. Women eat that stuff up. That's why we pay you to keep writing them."

"It's different in person. I found that out with Jen. Jen expected me to be that way all the time, along with hanging out with friends and going to parties and, well, I ran out of juice for a while because of that. I don't want to do that again."

"Has she shown any indication that's what she has in mind?"

"No, but in the beginning, neither did Jen."

"Okay, I get that. But Carrie is not Jen. They don't sound like they're anything alike."

"No, they aren't. Hell, Carrie can even cook! She made chocolate pie for me. Oh, my God to die for chocolate pie. I could've plunged face first into that pie, but of course I held back and ate a piece like a normal human. Jen never did anything remotely like that."

"All right, besides being a good cook, how else is she different?"

"She doesn't look anything like her. She rides her bike every day. Jen wouldn't have been caught dead on a bicycle or running. She was a tennis player who was mostly into it for the cute outfits."

"So...Carrie doesn't look like Jen. She doesn't act like Jen. What's the issue here? Just because Jen turned into a jerk, do you think every other woman in the world is going to be one, too? If so, you're looking at a long, lonely life my friend." AJ pulled off her marshmallows and popped them into her mouth.

Shawn sat back down and stared at her empty beer bottle.

"What're you thinking?" AJ strung two more marshmallows onto her stick and held them to the fire.

"I'm thinking I've been an idiot. I did something stupid."

"You mean something else stupid?"

"Yes, I mean something else. I couldn't sleep with Carrie. I was afraid of what it'd mean if we did. I mean, you don't just jump into bed with someone like her and have it mean nothing other than a romp."

"Okay, so what did you do?" AJ took the empty bottle from Shawn and handed her a full one. "This is getting good!"

"Oh, no, it's not. It's getting awful."

"I'm waiting. Spill it." AJ wiggled her eyebrows.

"A friend of a friend. Tracy. She's a photographer. She's cute and very sexy and she came on to me. She said she wanted to talk about collaborating on a book she wants to do. Anyway, she invited me over."

"Wait. This is after you've been out with Carrie?" AJ pulled her nearly burned marshmallows out of the fire and blew on them. She popped them into her mouth and tossed her stick back into the fire staring at Shawn the whole time.

"Actually, after we had double dated."

"Oh, good grief." AJ took a sip out of her beer and leaned back in her chair, but her eyes were still glued to Shawn's face.

"Yeah, well, she gave me her business card, wrote her cell number on it and a note that made it clear she was interested."

"And..."

"And I called her a couple of days before I left. I told myself I was going there to talk business."

"Uh, huh...and did you?"

"Talk business? Yes, well, sort of. For about ten minutes, maybe. Then we had a couple of drinks and dinner."

"So far, nothing wrong."

"Then we had a couple more drinks."

"Uh, oh..." AJ leaned forward in her chair.

"Yeah, well, then I told her how nice the view is from her patio and she said something about the view being even prettier from upstairs. Once I got up there, I found she meant the view from her bedroom. The whole outside wall of her bedroom is one huge window."

"Oh...boy..." AJ shook her head slowly.

"Oh boy is right. Well, the view from the second floor really is astounding, especially in the evening with the lights from across the river reflecting on the water and all that. We stood there in the dark enjoying the view. The next thing I know, she's really coming on to me...you know, the whole 'it would be so much nicer to enjoy with someone here all night' and that kind of stuff. Her hands are roaming all over and my God it had been so long, and well, I sort of remember being led to the bed. The next thing I remember is waking up in her bed nearly naked with her draped over me, completely naked."

"Are you telling me you had a hot night with that woman and don't remember a thing?"

Shawn nodded slowly. "Pretty much. I felt awful the next morning. She seemed pretty happy, so I guess it wasn't bad. She made me breakfast, but I didn't feel much like eating anything. Between the headache and just plain feeling stupid, I really just wanted to go home."

"Seriously, you don't remember anything about what you two did?"

"No, but it's pretty clear something did happen. We were both in her bed, naked, and she was cuddled up to me, like I said. Doesn't that suggest that we..."

"Yeah, I'd say that was pretty suggestive. But doesn't prove anything. Still, if you did sleep with her when you were stuck on Carrie, that doesn't sound good. Carrie doesn't know, does she?"

Shawn sighed. "I didn't tell her, if that's what you're asking. I wasn't that stupid. I called you the same morning and asked to come up."

"I get it. But didn't you say anything to Carrie before you left?"

"I saw Carrie that night, though I didn't tell her anything about seeing Tracy. She had made a chocolate pie. Do you believe that? No way could she know that's my favorite, but it is. Every time I'm near her I can feel something between us. Something more than just a few kisses. I feel like I might be falling in love with her. But I'm so afraid of going through the same thing again. I was really stuck on Jen, too."

"Let's go through this again. Jen and Carrie do not sound like they're anything alike. Carrie, on the other hand, sounds like someone who'd be very good for you. She obviously likes you very much. You care about her. What's wrong? She doesn't have a former lover who is twice your size and lives a few more houses away, does she?"

Shawn laughed softly. "No. Nothing like that."

"Well, what then? Why on God's green earth are you doing this to yourself and to her?"

"I guess I just don't want to be hurt again." AJ kicked Shawn in the foot. "Ow! Yeah, I know, I should be a little more thick-skinned, but I'm not."

"Maybe, just maybe, that's one of the things that makes you a really good writer."

"What, that I'm some kind of romantic idiot?" Shawn stared at AJ.

"No, that you feel things a little more than some people. That you care about hurting Carrie as well. Have you called her since you left?"

"I did. I called her the night I got to your place. Then the next day I sent her some flowers. Nothing big, just a little 'thinking of you' present."

"Good start. Sounds to me like you need to make a new beginning with Carrie. Just start over again when you get back. That's if she'll go for that."

Shawn sighed again, leaned back in the chair, and stared at the stars. "Funny, that thing with Tracy was so easy, but felt so wrong. Several times with Carrie, I wanted to make love to her so very much, but just couldn't. I knew that with Carrie, it meant something. With Tracy, it meant nothing really...just a good time for an evening. I want it to mean something. I want to make love, not just have sex. Not that there's anything wrong with that, either. Hell, Carrie even told me the night before I left that she wanted me. She does things to me just by being in the room. The smell of her shampoo makes me nuts."

AJ smiled and shook her head. "You have it bad. Just give in, buddy. Look, no one can say that anything will last forever. Wouldn't you rather take a chance with Carrie and enjoy whatever happens, rather than running away and never knowing how happy you could be with her?"

Shawn stared into the fire. "I'm beginning to think so. I think I needed to talk this out with you, knowing that you'd probably kick my butt. I also think that you're the best kind of friend anyone could have."

"Yeah, I love you, too."

"But not like that!" they said together, laughing.

"All right, here's a plan. Tomorrow, we'll go into the village. And while we're there, you need to call Carrie. Even if you just talk to her for a few minutes, you need to talk to her. It's up to you whether you tell her what you did, but if I were you, I'd tell her."

"Really? Are you sure?" Shawn looked stricken, her stomach suddenly turned to a hard knot.

"Really. Think about it. There's a chance she'll find out anyway. Wouldn't you rather she heard it from you than from someone else? Besides, how do you know she hasn't already heard? Better you bring it up and tell her your version of the story than for her to bring it up and you spend a lot of time backpedaling, trying to explain."

"I guess so," Shawn said. "Besides, if she is mad at me, she can't throw anything at me through the phone. Seriously, that could be the make or break of this whole thing. What if she hates me and never wants to see me again?"

"You're the romance writer. Write yourself a great scene. Write yourself the grand gesture. Write yourself a better ending than that. Come on, you can do it. Fight for what you want. Carrie sounds like she's worth fighting for."

"She is." Shawn leaned forward with her elbows on her knees, her chin cradled in her hands, once more staring into the fire. "She definitely is."

CHAPTER TWENTY-NINE

IT HAD BEEN A few days since Carrie had received the flowers from Shawn. There had been no further contact, and she wondered what Shawn was doing. She was wondering whether she'd hear from her again before she just turned up again at her house, when her phone rang and she saw Shawn's name in the Caller ID.

"Hi. Hope I'm not interrupting anything uninterruptable," Shawn said.

"Oh, no, just working at my desk. No one's in the office but me today. How are you doing?" Carrie tried to sound nonchalant.

"We're fine. Camping out in the Smokies at an old cabin AJ has. We had to come back into civilization for more ice and some other stuff."

"I see. Having fun?"

"Yeah, just chilling, mostly. We've done a little hiking but mostly it's been just communing with nature and relaxing. It's very nice here, with all the trees and quiet. Uh, I was thinking you might enjoy coming up here some time."

"It sounds like a great place. I used to camp with my grandparents, but that was a long time ago," Carrie said. "You and your friend staying out of trouble?"

"Oh yeah. Not much to get into trouble with, around here. It's pretty far out into the boonies. There's not even a phone signal unless you come closer to town, so that rules out e-mails and texting, too."

"No pretty girls up there bothering you guys?"

"Not unless some of these pesky squirrels are girls. We haven't even seen a bear yet, either, but believe me, I'm good with that. Speaking of pesky girls, I need to talk to you about something."

Carrie took a deep breath. *Here it comes, whatever it is.* "Okay."

"I did something I'm not proud of. I did something I shouldn't have, and before I tell you what it is, I'm going to tell you I'm sorry up front."

Carrie almost started to laugh. *Shawn really doesn't know what happened with Tracy. Serious, Carrie, be serious.* "Okay. What did you do that you think you need to apologize to me for? We didn't do anything for you to be sorry for." She tried to focus on restacking some papers on her desk, but it wasn't working.

"I know. We didn't do anything. I did something," Shawn took a deep breath. "I slept with Tracy. Now, before you get angry and hang up, I want you to know I was drunk, and I don't remember anything about it. That's no excuse, but I wanted to tell you before you heard it from Tracy or Kelly. I'm so sorry."

Carrie had to put her hand over her mouth to keep from giggling into the phone. *Poor Shawn, she really is feeling awful about this. As well she should. Maybe she should suffer just a bit longer.*

"Look, you and I don't have an exclusive relationship. How do you know I didn't sleep with someone else after we started seeing each other?"

"Did you?" Shawn's voice was just above a whisper.

Carrie made her wait as she paused for effect. "No, I didn't. I could've, though, since I don't have a claim on you or you on me other than good friends, right?" She could feel Shawn squirm on the other end.

"Uh, no, I guess not. I guess I sort of thought…"

"What did you sort of think?" Carrie asked softly.

"Well, I guess from things you said…"

Time to give it up, Carrie thought. "Shawn, I haven't been with anyone since we met. Except you. You're still the one I want."

"You do? Even after what I told you? Are you sure?"

"Yes, I do. I can't wait forever for you to figure out when you'll be ready to move on to something more with me. I'm hoping you'll get your issues, whatever they are, worked out up there in the woods. Maybe the higher altitude will help."

"My head is feeling clearer already. Then you forgive me for what I did?"

"If that's what you need from me, yes. I forgive you for what you did. By the way, I had Kelly over a couple of days ago."

"Kelly? Really?"

"Yes, really. I made lunch for her. We had a great time. Tracy has a new girlfriend, some sculptor from Fort Myers Beach named Chris. Nice, but not my type."

"You met Tracy's new girlfriend?"

"Oh yeah, didn't I tell you? I was at Kelly's for a cookout. Let's see, there was me, Kelly, Tracy and Chris. It was fun. Tracy made a point of chatting me up about you when we were alone for a few minutes. I hope you don't mind that I told them you're out of town."

"No, that was okay. I didn't tell them. They probably wondered where I am, right?"

"Pretty much, yeah."

"Anything else happen?" Carrie could almost hear Shawn holding her breath.

Carrie was ready to drop the bomb. "Tracy told me you spent the night with her."

There was silence from the other end for a few seconds, before Shawn said softly, "Well, I guess you've got the story from both ends now. I'm glad you aren't mad at me."

"I didn't say I wasn't mad at you. I said I didn't have an exclusive claim on you, nor do you have one on me…at least not yet. I was still hurt that you would do something like that, even if you had a few too many drinks. I guess what made me feel worst was that you could find yourself in her bed, but not mine. I sort of thought maybe we had something going, but again, I don't have a claim on you."

"Carrie, I do want you. You know I do. I didn't…I mean I wouldn't…I mean, hell, I don't know what to say. I was an idiot. I don't even remember what happened. That's pretty bad, isn't it?"

"I would say so."

"Uh, you know Kelly has a crush on you."

"Yes, I know. And?"

"And, so…" Shawn ran her hand through her hair, trying to figure out how to ask. "So did you and Kelly…? Don't bother answering that, since it's none of my business."

"Right this minute, no, it isn't. But no, nothing is going on. I was sort of her date for the cookout at her house. Then I asked her to lunch. That's it. We're just friends. Does that make you feel better?"

"Actually, yes," Shawn said, taking a deep breath. "Listen, I'll be coming home in about a week. Could we start over again? This time, I promise there won't be any ghosts coming back to haunt whatever happens with us."

"Shawn, I'm looking forward to seeing you again. That sounds like a great idea. Let's start over. Shall we meet at the end of my driveway again?" Carrie laughed.

"Let's see what happens. I'll give you a call when I'm on my way back, all right?"

"I'd like that. Bring me a pine cone from the Smokies?"

"You got it. I, uh, well...I'll talk to you again soon."

"Okay. Have a good time up there and a safe trip."

Carrie hung up, took a deep breath and smiled. She just couldn't tell Shawn what actually happened. Not yet. Someday she would tell her. Meantime, she had a nice, warm feeling inside. Shawn was coming back home and they would start over. Maybe now those demons she'd been battling were gone.

***

That night, the weather guys on television were talking about a depression in the Atlantic off the coast of Africa that was beginning to develop into a storm. It was that time of year, after all. Most of them shriveled away to nothing before they got to any land. Some decided to visit Florida. Grace was going to be one of those summer visitors. And she didn't know it yet, but she was headed for Fort Myers.

CHAPTER THIRTY

A FEW DAYS LATER, Rich and Carrie were having coffee in the break room. "So I guess you heard about Tropical Storm Grace?" Rich asked.

Carrie nodded. "Yes, I decided last night to recheck my supplies. I always check my hurricane kit at the beginning of the season, just to be sure. Never want to be running around looking for batteries or the like when everyone else is. How about you, are you stocked up, too?" She reached for her coffee cup.

"Yeah. Karen grew up in Key West. She knows what to do, so I leave it for her unless she tells me she needs me to do something."

"It's nice to be able to depend on someone else, isn't it? I mean, you don't have to deal with everything yourself. If you need to put up the hurricane shutters, you even have help."

Rich laughed. "True. She can wield a wicked power drill. She could probably put them all up by herself, not being the 'little woman' type at all. I couldn't have a wife like that. She's a true partner in every sense of the word. But I usually take care of most of that. She says she leaves me the 'manly stuff' so my testosterone gets a workout."

"Karen's a smart woman. You know, I liked her the first time I met her. You guys sure are a good pair. I hope I find someone to partner with like you two are someday."

"You will," Rich said. "By the way, if this thing does head for us, and you need help shuttering your house, let me know. I can get a crew over there and get it all done in no time."

"I'll keep that in mind. Seems like last year we only had one scare, if I remember correctly but that's all it was. Nothing very serious. Never know, this might just turn into a 'watch' thing more than a real warning."

"Speaking of serious. Have you heard from Shawn?"

"I have. She's camping in the Smokies with her publisher. I talked to her a couple of days ago."

Rich raised his eyebrows and took a sip from his coffee. "And?"

"And...she'll be home in a while. She said she'll call when she's on her way." Carrie smiled, and then took a sip from her mug.

"Does she know about Grace?"

"I doubt it. I didn't know about it, either, when I last talked to her. She said she wasn't getting a phone signal at all up there unless they drove to the village several miles away. I'm assuming she still doesn't know, but I'll tell her the next time she calls. Speaking of needing help, she probably will. Her house is bigger than mine by half with that addition you've put on."

"True. Well, the offer goes for her, too. I wouldn't want to take a chance on all that handsome work we did getting ruined. Tell her what I said when you talk to her, okay? If you don't hear from her in time, we'll just go over and shutter her house for her anyway."

"I will." Carrie got up and headed for the sink with her cup.

Rich went for a coffee refill to take back to his office. As Carrie reached the door back to the front office, he said, "Carrie, you seem happier than I've seen you for a while. Things going well?"

"They are. Thanks for asking." Carrie smiled at her boss. "I think they'll be getting even better soon." She turned and walked back to her desk, humming.

CHAPTER THIRTY-ONE

IT HAD BEEN NEARLY a week since Shawn had talked to Carrie. She and AJ spent their time hiking all over the area, staying up late talking about everything from the world's problems to debating the best hiking socks. And they talked about Shawn and Carrie.

"You so need to get out of here and go back to Florida," AJ said one morning as they sat outside with their breakfast.

"What makes you think that?" Shawn asked, in between bites of the bacon she held in her fingers.

"Seems like almost everything we talk about has something to do with Carrie, that's what. I know you came up here for a good time and to relax. Okay, you also came to spend time with me. Right now, though, you need to get back home and take care of things with her. I bet you're ready to go, aren't you?"

"I guess so. I'm sorry about talking about her so much. Actually, I don't think I'm sorry at all, but I guess you're right. Now that I know she doesn't hate me for what happened, and I don't feel like I'm going to run away again. I can hardly wait to get back there and start over."

"Well, then, let's pack up right after breakfast and get out of here. I wouldn't mind getting back to civilization and a nice hot shower. Besides, the women in Atlanta probably miss me." AJ laughed. "God knows I miss them."

"Now that's probably true. Besides, I can testify that you need a shower."

"Look who's talking! You could use one too, believe me. Bathing in the creek just isn't the same, is it?"

On the way back toward civilized territory, Shawn kept an eye on her cell, watching for a connection. Finally, she saw a couple of bars, then another, show up on her screen. She finally had an adequate looking connection and asked AJ to pull over for a couple of minutes at the nearest turnout. A couple of miles farther and they found it. Shawn got out of the truck and sat on a guard rail to make her call.

"Carrie, hi. Miss me?"

"Of course I do. I miss you a lot. Now there's something else going on. Have you heard that Hurricane Grace is headed in this direction?"

"Hurricane? The last news I heard was that it was a depression. That was several days ago now. That thing developed fast! Are we in the cone?" Shawn asked, referring to the directional possibility cone the weather stations use.

"The Weather Channel is showing us in the path, in the 'pretty sure' area of the cone. WINK news says we're on the edge of possible hurricane force winds, but if it turns, of course, it could be much worse. The good thing is that Rich shuttered your house just in case, since we didn't know when you were coming home. Maybe you should just stay in Atlanta till it's over."

"We're leaving the Smokies today. I should be home in a couple of days. I'll get there as quickly as I can. Wow, this has to happen while I'm gone, of course. Well, I was already coming home. I'm rambling, aren't I?"

"Well, yes, you are. But that's okay. Rich said to tell you he hoped you didn't mind that he shuttered your house without permission. He didn't want all that work he and his crew just finished to get messed up."

"Please thank him for me. I never stop being amazed at how people take care of each other when something happens. By the way, I'm sitting on a guardrail at a turnout along a two lane mountain road. It's picturesque, but we probably should get going."

"Okay. We'll know more tomorrow about which way the storm is tracking. You know how these things go, it's headed right for you then it veers off and you barely get any rain at all."

"All right, then, I'll call you tomorrow." Shawn paused. In a lower voice, she said, "Take care of yourself, all right?"

"You, too. Talk to you tomorrow."

Shawn smiled as she hung up. This felt good. Carrie felt good. She couldn't wait to get back home and she wasn't going to let a little hurricane get in the way.

CHAPTER THIRTY-TWO

CARRIE WAS STARTLED OUT of a good dream. Her phone was ringing. Glancing at the clock as she reached for the phone, she realized it was only five thirty. She took a quick look at Caller ID to make sure it wasn't some stupid wrong number, but instead, it was Shawn. She grabbed the phone and answered it.

"Shawn, what's going on? Are you okay?" She sat up quickly, rubbing her eyes and yawning.

"I'm fine, but I'm tired. I got up really early to get on the road. I'm sorry I just realized how early it still is."

"Yeah, it's pretty early, but that's all right. Where are you now?"

"I'm just south of Macon."

"Wow, you did get up early! What possessed you to do that? Scratch that...I'm sorry. But the storm is still a ways off. Nothing much new since I talked to you yesterday."

"So you haven't seen the news yet, then," Shawn said.

"Not yet. Why?"

"It's changed direction, moving more toward us and it's moving faster. They're saying it's going to make landfall somewhere near Fort Myers."

"Oh no. Last I'd heard it had veered away a bit and was headed more toward the Gulf. We were going to get just the outer edges of it as it passed. Hang on." Carrie reached for the television remote and flipped to the twenty-four hour weather station. There she was, Hurricane Grace, tracking more to the northeast, with the red cone pointed right toward Naples and Fort Myers now.

"I see it. Why aren't you staying in Atlanta? This thing might get too much for you to get home. I know these things can change direction again, but this one's looking pretty sure. Your house is safe, you know. And so am I."

"Carrie, I need to be home. I just feel like I should be there.

But…mainly, I just want to be home with you."

"Look, I'd love to have you here too, but don't get in a wreck or take chances trying to get here in time. Just being selfish, I want to see you get here in one piece." Carrie leaned back on her pillow with the phone to her ear. She smiled faintly. Talking to Shawn while in bed seemed rather intimate and nice, comfy, and sort of sexy even if they were discussing a hurricane.

"I plan to do just that. I should be back in seven, maybe eight hours, unless there's more construction or horrible traffic going south. If they set up an evacuation route, I might have trouble getting all the way there on I-75. I can call you later and let you know more about when I'll be there."

"Look, if you insist on doing this, I'd like that. As I said, your house is all closed up, so come straight to my house. If it doesn't look like you'll get here in time, please don't worry. I'll be fine. I'm all set and just waiting for it to get here."

"I know. I just want to be with you and start our starting over. Besides, I've been eating camping food for over a week, so going through a hurricane won't be a big deal to my stomach anyway. I know this is going to sound like a funny thing to ask right now, but by any chance, do you think there might be a chocolate pie?" She could picture Shawn grinning, waiting for the answer.

"Well, there could be. Hmm…there could be. There just might be. You don't happen to like chocolate pie, do you? Seems like I know someone who lives down the street who likes chocolate pie, too," Carrie teased.

"Well, I do declare," Shawn said, in her best southern belle accent. "I believe you have me down." She went back to her normal voice. "Actually, I'd love some, but you probably don't have time to do that today. I'll call you later at a much more decent hour and update you on where I am."

"Please take care of yourself and drive carefully."

"I will. Hope you can go back to sleep now."

"I'll try. Talk to you later," Carrie said, and hung up. "I miss you very much," she said to the 'call ended' cell screen. Then she rolled over in bed and hugged her pillow, drifting back to sleep smiling.

CHAPTER THIRTY-THREE

CARRIE TICKED OFF THE list of things in her head that she wanted to be sure were taken care of in case they lost power during the storm. Every piece of laundry clean. Check. Big bag of ice in the freezer for later. Check. Hurricane lamps filled with oil. Check. Lots of matches. Check. Propane stove ready. Check. Her generator was also all set, with extra gas cans. It wouldn't run the refrigerator. It wasn't big enough. But it would run some fans and some other things that could make life more comfortable if the power was lost. Yes, she was ready.

She had just sat down at the kitchen table with a cup of coffee when her cell went off. "Hey, Shawn. How's your drive going? You must be getting close to Florida by now."

"Hey yourself." Carrie could hear her take a sip from her soda. "Good guess. I'm just south of Valdosta. Actually, the traffic hasn't been too bad. I found some breakfast at a drive-through a while ago and I've been making good time…I probably shouldn't have called you earlier. It was way too early and I apologize for that."

"No problem. I honestly didn't mind. In fact, I'm glad you called me." Carrie took a deep breath and smiled, remembering lying in bed talking to Shawn earlier. "At this rate you'll be back in town by early afternoon for sure. Well, unless they order evacuations. Then you might have a problem. The authorities have already told people on the islands to prepare to leave, but that shouldn't cause a problem. It's looking pretty sure for Grace to come straight here. You're going to cut it really close. Seriously, why don't you just stay up there until it passes?"

"I have to try, Carrie. I'd much rather be there and go through the storm with you. I'll call you later. I'm so looking forward to being home and seeing you."

"I'm looking forward to seeing you, too, but I'd rather you didn't take chances."

"I promise I won't take any big chances. I'm sure I can make it if the storm can just not speed up. You'll let me know if anything significant happens, right?"

"I will. Just be careful." Carrie hit end on her phone and smiled again. She felt warm all over, straight to her core, in anticipation. She tried not to let her imagination run completely wild, but she couldn't help fantasizing just a little—no, quite a bit—about riding out the storm with Shawn. There'd be nothing to do but to be together.

* * *

Shawn smiled as she passed the 'Welcome to Florida' sign on I-75. *If all went well, by early to mid-afternoon she'd be home. Well, she'd be at Carrie's. Carrie's, what a nice thought.* Then her conscience began beating her up again. *You acted like a complete and total idiot. You almost ruined everything.* She took a deep breath and tried to figure out what kind of gesture she should make to help straighten out what she did before she left. One thing was for sure no more messing around with Tracy and she could find someone else if she was serious about doing that photography book.

As she drove on through the morning, the sun climbed higher in the sky, and the day became warmer and stickier. A couple of times she rolled the window down, just to get some fresh air into the Jeep, but that never lasted long. It was too warm and muggy by ten in the morning even for riding down the Interstate at seventy-five miles per hour with the windows down.

She was keeping up with the big trucks and passing some. She realized she was paying much more attention to the traffic on the way home than she had on the way up to Atlanta. On the way up, she had been fleeing and only thought of getting away. On the way home, all she could think about was going home, and home right now meant getting back to Carrie.

As she drove, she played out in her mind what she'd say, what she'd do when she saw Carrie again. *Should I pretend that nothing has happened? Should I try to be funny and make a joke about the weather? What I want to do is drop my bags on the floor inside the door and reach out for Carrie. I want to hold her and kiss her and tell her how much I missed her. I want to show her how much I care about her, and this time not stop until I've made sweet love to her. Oh yes, that's exactly what I want to do. But so not a good thing to contemplate in detail while driving. Oh no.* She wished she could show up with at least a bouquet of flowers. Nothing big, even a small bunch of flowers from Publix would be good. But even that wasn't going to happen. She had to go straight there. The storm was coming.

About eleven thirty she found a McDonalds next to a Racetrack station along the Interstate and pulled in for a quick pit stop. A full gas tank, fast bathroom trip, a couple of hamburgers and a large Coke with extra ice, and she was back on the road, closing on home by the minute. She called Carrie one more time as she pulled out of McDonald's.

"Well, I'm almost there," Shawn said when Carrie answered. "I just picked up a light lunch. Next stop home, I think."

"I'm glad to hear that. I'll be even happier to see you pulling into my driveway."

"Oh, me, too. Definitely looking forward to that. I'm making good time, so I should be in North Fort Myers by about one thirty or two. You know, I don't mind driving, but this is tiring."

"You were up pretty early this morning, too. Glad you're holding up so far."

"I am, but I'll probably collapse once I get there. At least for a while. But for now, I'm just entertaining myself with thoughts of you and a nice warm shower. Pretty much in that order."

"Yes, a nice warm shower and maybe a nap would be something to look forward to." Carrie's grin evident in her voice.

"Looking forward to seeing you actually is keeping my brain working right now. I can't wait to see you."

"I'm looking forward to seeing you, too," Carrie said softly. "I've been thinking about that since we last talked."

Shawn made a dramatic sighing noise, then chuckled. "I guess I'd better pay attention to the road. This kind of talk makes my mind lose contact with what I'm doing. Don't forget you're talking to someone who makes up stories for a living. I have a very vivid imagination."

"Imagine away, but stay focused on the road, please. I'm sure we can do something about that when you get here, though. Oh, by the way, it's getting breezy and overcast, but it looks like the storm has slowed down just a little bit. It appears you have a bit more time to get here, so you don't have to drive quite so fast or worry."

"Okay, thanks for the info. That makes it a bit easier."

"I'd better get back to work, myself."

"Work? Aren't you at home?"

"I am at home, but a pie wants to be made. I already have everything I need, but it won't make itself. Besides, it would be nice to snack on during the storm. See? I can rationalize even making a pie. Call me when you're closer?"

"Will do. See you in a while." Shawn grinned widely as she punched the button on her phone, pitched it into the passenger seat, and decided she had better find some better music on the radio to keep her mind on the road.

CHAPTER THIRTY-FOUR

IT WAS NEARLY TWO by the time Carrie took the pie crust out of the oven. She wanted it to be perfect, and it definitely had that golden brown look, like you'd want to eat it all by itself. The chocolate pudding filling would go in shortly and then the meringue, then back into the oven for a few more minutes. But in the meantime, Shawn could be there any minute.

Carrie had changed her clothes three times while the crust was baking, finally deciding on a pair of white shorts and lavender tank top. She didn't think she had been this nervous the other times Shawn had been there, but this time was different. Before, other than those wow kisses, she just had fantasies about Shawn. Now, well, it's possible some of those fantasies could actually happen.

Shawn was coming to her. She sounded different. She was acting differently. She wanted to be with her. They were going to start over. And they were going to spend quality time together. At least until the hurricane passed. Anything could happen, and she had definite ideas of what that anything should look like. Those hot kisses they shared before were just the beginning. She could almost feel Shawn's hands on her once again.

***

Shortly after two, Shawn pulled into Carrie's driveway and parked the Jeep as close to the house as she could. The queen palms on the street were waving wildly in the stiff breeze and rain was spitting hard at her as she grabbed her things out of the Jeep and practically ran to Carrie's door. Her mouth started to go dry. *What am I going to say to Carrie in person? Hi, thanks for having me over? Glad to see you? Should I kiss her at the door? Come on, Shawn! God, I do this for a living. What would one of my heroes do?*

Before Shawn could decide what to do, or even knock on the door, Carrie was opening it, looking radiant. Shawn was sure she had never seen anyone look lovelier. Was that a word? Didn't matter. It fit. Time seemed to stop while they stared at each other. "Hi."

"Hi, yourself," Carrie said, holding the door open wider. "Come on in."

Once inside, she dropped her stuff and closed the door. Her back against the door, she took Carrie's hand and pulled her gently closer. She placed a soft kiss on Carrie's lips and whispered, "I have so looked forward to this." Shawn pulled her into an embrace and nuzzled into Carrie's hair, nearly drowning in the scent of her. *Oh, yes, this was what I have been waiting for.*

"Me, too," Carrie said, nestling into Shawn's arms.

Shawn placed a kiss on her forehead, and smiled as she stroked Carrie's back. She suddenly lost all her nervousness and just stood there holding Carrie. She felt her heart still beating fast, but it was no longer from nerves.

Carrie stepped away from Shawn's embrace, looking her in the eyes. What Shawn knew Carrie saw now was a calmness, a desire. Carrie reached back for Shawn and turned her face up to find Shawn's lips once more reaching for hers.

"Carrie..." Shawn whispered against Carrie's mouth. "I..."

Carrie silenced her with another kiss. Their lips met again with more intensity. Carrie's mouth admitted Shawn's tongue, which began a dance with hers, Carrie moaning in response. Their bodies pressed together, Shawn's hands roamed down Carrie's back to her behind, pulling her even closer. She deepened the kiss, answering Carrie's probing tongue with hers. Shawn could feel the heat of Carrie's body against hers. Everywhere their bodies touched felt like fire. She was being consumed. This time, Shawn didn't want to run. This time, she could feel the wall she had built start to crack, then crumble at the touch of one Carrie Alexander. This time, she let Carrie lead her to her bedroom.

If Shawn had had eyes for anything besides Carrie, she'd have noticed the white painted antique iron bed with the blue and white quilt, the old oak dresser, the standing mirror in the corner of the little bedroom. But she saw none of this. All she saw was Carrie and her gorgeous brown eyes as she reached for Shawn's shirt. But first, Shawn pulled Carrie's tank top over her head, revealing those breasts she had dreamed about held only in a pink lace bra. Her hands trembled slightly as she reached out to unhook the bra and release them, the pink lace dropping to the floor.

"Oh, God, Carrie," she moaned as her hands caressed her, causing a matching moan from Carrie.

Carrie pulled Shawn's polo shirt over her head, revealing Shawn's sports bra, which shortly came off as well. Carrie reached for the waist of Shawn's shorts, pulling her closer for another kiss, their tongues playing together. As the kiss deepened, they stood there, their breasts touching, Shawn's hands on Carrie's butt pulling her even closer.

Seemingly unable to stand it any longer, Carrie pulled away, reached for Shawn's shorts, quickly unbuttoned and unzipped them, pushing them and her boxers down in one move, leaving Shawn to step out of them and kick them aside. Shawn reached for Carrie's shorts, unzipped them and pushed them down, revealing the pink lace bikinis underneath. In one move, she then pushed them down and Carrie stepped out of them, revealing the rest of the curves Shawn had only dreamed about.

Finally completely skin-to-skin, their hands freely roamed, their mouths tasted. Shawn ran kisses down the soft skin below Carrie's ear to her collarbone as Carrie moaned her name. She continued the kisses to the silky swell of Carrie's breast, finally cupping it and suckling on the already erect nipple. She repeated this on her other breast, hearing Carrie whimper in response. Carrie began breathing even harder and Shawn gently guided her down onto the bed, crawling in after her.

"Carrie, you are so beautiful," she whispered as she continued the line of kisses down her tummy, pausing only when Carrie began giggling.

"I'm sorry, but I'm very ticklish on my stomach." Carrie grinned as she stroked Shawn's hair. "Please don't stop. Oh, God, that feels good."

Shawn grinned back, then softly stroked Carrie's thigh with her hand as she continued kissing her way down her body to her little triangle of curls. She reached for Carrie's slit, and moaned again as she felt her fully erect clit and the wetness below. Her mouth back on Carrie's, her fingers caressed her clit as Carrie pressed against her hand, matching her stroke for stroke.

"Please, I want to feel you inside," Carrie whispered against Shawn's lips, her breathing ragged.

Shawn obliged, with one finger into her wetness, then two, Carrie breathing sharply at each, then an "Oh yes, oh yes," as she moved steadily against Shawn's hand. Shawn claimed Carrie's mouth again as her hand claimed the rest of her. Carrie called out Shawn's name as she came, with Shawn nearly coming herself from hearing her. She rolled them over and pulled Carrie close, their bodies intertwined, but shortly

Carrie had other plans.

"Oh no, this isn't over." Looking into Shawn's eyes, Carrie caressed Shawn's face, placing soft kisses on her lips, her forehead, and then kissing her way down Shawn's chest. Shawn suddenly gasped and moaned as Carrie reached Shawn's breast, kissing her way to her nipple. Shawn reached for Carrie, bringing her back for kisses that deepened as their tongues danced once again. Carrie's hands continued their exploration of Shawn's tummy. Her fingers reached the soft skin inside Shawn's thighs, trailing her hand gently against them and ultimately arriving at the soft curls where they met.

Shawn moaned into Carrie's mouth as Carrie's hand cupped her and she felt fingers delve into her wetness. She began moving with Carrie's hand as their mouths claimed each other. Shawn reached for Carrie and once again her fingers slid into Carrie as they both reached their peak and tumbled over together.

Afterward, lying in Shawn's arms, Carrie listened to the pulse of Shawn's heart beating in her ear and the sound of their breathing as the downpour outside began in earnest. The steady pinging of rain on the metal roof and the whine of the wind around the house made her feel like they were the only two people in the world. She smiled and reached up to place a soft kiss on Shawn's lips. "What're you thinking about?"

"Mmm...thinking about how delicious you are." Shawn gazed into Carrie's eyes. "I can't believe I ran from this."

"Well, I sure can." Carrie laughed softly. "But wow, was the wait worth it! Oh, my God, that felt so good."

"It sure did. It feels so right to be here with you. So very perfect." Shawn sighed slowly, and softly stroked Carrie's cheek with her fingertips. "Right now I can't imagine being anywhere else in the world, and I'm so glad I got here in time. I couldn't wait to be here and show you how much I care for you."

"I care very much for you, too. You make me crazy, but you also make me feel like no one else ever has. This feels very right to me, too." Carrie cuddled just a little closer, her leg across Shawn's thigh, her toes softly playing up and down her calf, listening to Shawn's breathing slow as she fell asleep.

Carrie sighed. The wind was now howling around the house, but she knew the storm was still quite a ways off the coast. *Bring it on, Grace. Let's get this over with.* She snuggled a little closer to Shawn, her head on Shawn's chest, and dozed off smiling.

CHAPTER THIRTY-FIVE

SHAWN CAUGHT A WHIFF of something wonderful as she opened her eyes. There was pretty much no doubt what it was, but as Carrie walked past the bedroom door, she called out. "By any chance do I smell chocolate pie?"

Carrie looked through the door, came in and sat on the side of the bed. "Well, look who's up! As a matter of fact, you do." She placed a soft kiss on Shawn's lips. "Did you have a nice nap?"

"I did. That felt so nice. All of it did." Shawn smiled a sleepy smile, her eyes still half closed.

"Well, I figured since the power was still on I'd finish that pie I started earlier. I've started supper, too. Why don't you go take that shower you wanted, then come to the kitchen and keep me company?"

"Mmm...sounds like a great idea."

Shawn stretched, crawled out of bed, and took a quick shower before putting her clothes back on. She smiled as she remembered what was happening when those things came off just a few hours ago. Once she was dressed, she wandered into the kitchen, came up behind Carrie, and put her arms around Carrie's waist. Carrie leaned back into Shawn's arms with a little sigh.

"Oh, that feels good," she said. "So is this a 'kiss the cook' thing?"

Shawn left a little kiss on the back of Carrie's neck, then snuggled a little closer. "Maybe," she said. "But I've discovered you're much more talented than just cooking."

"Oh yeah?" Carrie said, turning around and putting her arms around Shawn's waist. She leaned into Shawn's embrace, her lips barely touching Shawn's ear, she whispered, "And what kind of talent would that be?"

"Oh, my God, Carrie," Shawn murmured, barely able to keep her knees from buckling. She swallowed hard. "Do you have any idea what you're doing to me?"

"I sure hope so, at least that's the idea," Carrie whispered again against Shawn's ear. She pulled away a bit and left a soft little kiss on Shawn's lips. "Hold that thought till after supper. We'd better eat while we can still have something warm. Why don't you go sit at the table and talk to me."

Shawn took a seat at the little kitchen table. She couldn't help herself. She kept staring at Carrie. She wanted to touch her. Everything about Carrie suddenly seemed important...the way she held a spoon, the little piece of hair that had escaped her ponytail, the tiny freckle on the back of her left knee. Shawn drank in every single thing about her.

As if she knew she was being scrutinized, Carrie turned around and caught Shawn's stare. "What?"

"What do you mean?"

"What are you staring at?" Carrie brushed the back of her shorts. "Is there something on me?"

"No, nothing. I was just admiring you. I'm sorry if I was being too obvious. I like looking at you."

Carrie's face turned a bit pink, right down her neck to her tank top, even as she grinned back at Shawn. She turned back to the stove, picked up the dish of scalloped potatoes, and without looking at Shawn, placed it on the table. She did the same with the plate of ham she took from the oven and the dish of green beans. Carrie brought the biscuits to the table last, and finally looked over at her.

"Dig in. I hope you aren't too tired to eat. I know you've had a very long drive today, not to mention how busy you were after you got here." She grinned.

Shawn raised her eyebrows suggestively. "Yes, we were both busy after I got here, weren't we?" She didn't need an answer and she didn't need a second invitation to reach for a spoon. "And yeah, it was a long drive, but so worth it. All I wanted to do was get back here in time. I couldn't stand the thought of you here and me there during this storm. I haven't eaten since that early lunch on the road." She dished out several spoons full of potatoes. "This looks and smells so good."

"It was nothing...Well, a little something. I had already decided to cook some of what was in my fridge. This is one of those hurricane meals we had as kids. You know, where Mom cooked up anything that might go bad while the power was off. The pie was something special I made for you, but the rest, well, it was just supper. I'd planned to do this anyway, but it's nicer you're here to share it with. And it'll be even better to have you here with me to go through the storm."

As if on cue, the lights flickered, and then went out. Carrie lit a couple of hurricane lamps, put one on the table and one on the kitchen counter before sitting down to eat like nothing happened. Shawn looked over at Carrie, her face aglow from the lamp, and wondered how she could ever have doubted that she was the one.

"You look beautiful in lamplight," Shawn said, and then realized she hadn't said it out loud. She sighed, picked up her fork, and speared a piece of ham.

Carrie just smiled.

"I was just out at BJ's yesterday afternoon." Carrie reached for a biscuit. "I was glad to see there wasn't anyone grabbing up all the bottled water or batteries. You'd think it was just another day. I noticed even the gas prices have not gone up. I noticed the same thing at Publix as well."

"That's a good sign," Shawn said, in between mouthfuls of scalloped potatoes.

"Either people were just not panicking, or a lot of them were figuring on taking off for higher ground when it hit. By the way, have you talked to Kelly today?"

"Yeah, I talked to her this morning while I was driving. She was pretty much all set. She did say, though, that she knew several people who were evacuating. Some because they'll be required to, and some because they have little kids who are already scared because they went through Hurricane Christy last year. Guess it scared them enough they didn't want to be here for this storm. Speaking of evacuating, Greg texted me that he was one of the evacuees from the beach area. He took off for Georgia, to his dad's. That's his standard evacuation plan."

"Oh good," Carrie said. "I wondered how he was, but assumed he knew what to do and would be safe."

"Oh yeah, Greg's been living at the beach long enough to know when to get out. It's part of living there. You know, I always wondered where people went when they evacuated if they didn't have family to go to. Do they just drive until they feel safe and then go find a hotel where they can hole up until it's safe to come home?"

"I don't think I've ever really thought about that. Well, the interstates didn't seem to be overly clogged with cars going north today. According to the news, I-75 and I-95 were pretty busy for a while yesterday but that was because the Keys were under a mandatory evacuation."

"I heard on the news while I was driving that Marco Island, Sanibel and Captiva, and Fort Myers Beach are now under mandatory evacuation as well. That means Greg's out of there. It's the usual. Still, I feel bad for them," Shawn said.

"Well, at this point whoever had to get out is already out. No one should be out driving around at this point. It's too late to worry about anything now, just let it happen."

It was going to be a long night, and Shawn wondered why hurricanes always seemed to pass through in the dark like they were trying to sneak in. After supper, they watched out the open front door, since the windows all had the shutters latched down. The branches at the tops of trees were waving around to music only they could hear. The sky had become a bit greyer, but it was hard to tell at that point. Grey was grey. Rain was coming down pretty hard, but these were still just the outer rain bands, and it was going to get actually dark soon.

Just then, the power flickered, then came back on again, and Carrie extinguished the hurricane lamps. With nothing else to do, they watched movies in between looking out the front door and checking the Weather Channel to see what was happening. Shawn checked the charge on all her electronics, including their cell phones, ready for when the power went back off again.

CHAPTER THIRTY-SIX

SHAWN PLOPPED DOWN ON the sofa after handing Carrie a bottle of Pepsi. "Anything new while I was out of the room?"

"They're now estimating landfall will be just after midnight, but at this point, who knows."

"Yeah, it's definitely going to be a long night. Hey, remember going through hurricanes when you were a kid? The air would get so humid that it felt like you'd leave a wake in the air like a boat through water." Shawn shook her head slowly. "That was so nasty. But that's just the way it was. At least nowadays we have battery-powered fans for during the storm, and generators for afterward."

"Yes, I do remember. It was awful after the hurricane when there was no air conditioning and you'd just sit or lie there in the sweltering heat, fanning yourself with whatever you could grab. Whoever invented battery-powered fans should get a medal. Back then my dad would remind us again and again that's what it was like for everyone who lived here before there was air conditioning. He'd talk about that the whole time the power was off, trying to make us feel like pioneers, when all we wanted was to sit in front of a fan, and dry out a bit."

"Yeah, us, too." Shawn went back to typing something on her laptop.

"I'm going to be nosey, and ask you what you're working on." Carrie leaned to look over Shawn's shoulder.

"I decided to keep a hurricane diary." She turned the laptop around for Carrie to see. "Could be useful for something I write someday."

"I guess everything that happens to you could be useful someday, huh? Do you think of every experience as something that might be in a story?"

"Well, sort of. I guess that's just the way my brain works. Never know when you might need to call up some memory to get through part of a story. I'm thinking about putting my next book here in Florida, and a hurricane could happen to them, too."

"Good idea. Just remember that they need to stock up before the storm and they must have a hurricane kit in their house way before it happens. Or maybe you'd rather have your characters do dumb stuff like having a hurricane party and try to figure out how to deal with their stupidity later. I guess that would make a better story, wouldn't it?"

"That's an idea. If this thing hadn't caught me off guard, I'd have been readier. Is that a word? Anyway, I do own some supplies, and we can get into them if we need to afterward."

"And I've got a generator and you don't." Carrie teased her.

"And you have a generator and I don't," Shawn grinned back at her. "Yet. So I'm after you for your generator now, not just your luscious kissing?" Shawn teased back and leaned over and lightly kissed Carrie, then grinned some more.

"Could be. Never know. By the way, did you notice how everywhere you went yesterday, once you got closer, the last thing people said to each other was 'stay safe'?"

"Now that you mention it, yes, I did. Even when I stopped at McDonalds north of here."

"I think I noticed it more after Charley came through. It was so awful, it made an impression. Maybe it made people think about hurricanes differently. It's almost like when something like this happens everyone becomes related like cousins. The clerk at the grocery store or at the gas station, or wherever you talk to someone here, the last thing they say to you is 'stay safe'. Funny, I don't particularly remember that from being a kid here, but I probably wouldn't have noticed anyway."

"I keep thinking I can hear the rain letting up, but when I go over to the door to look out, I don't see anything different. Must be just the wind gusts off and on. I'd just like to get this over with. I hate the waiting part."

"Well..." Carrie ran her hand up Shawn's arm. "Maybe we could find something to do while we wait, besides eating, that is."

"Hmm...not a bad idea." Shawn made an elaborate play of closing her laptop, slowly. "What do you have in mind?" She reached for Carrie, but Carrie jumped up and took off toward the bedroom, laughing.

"Come take a nap with me!"

Shawn followed Carrie into the bedroom, visions of 'napping' making her ache. *Oh, yeah, let's nap.* She found Carrie sitting in the middle of the bed, grinning. Shawn stopped at the foot of the bed, trying to look serious.

"So you want to nap?" Shawn tried to control her grin. "I guess that could be arranged." She walked slowly around the foot of the white iron bed, then flopped down on one side of the bed without taking her eyes off Carrie. She held out her arms to Carrie, who snuggled into Shawn's shoulder.

Shawn sighed deeply. "How nappish are you?"

Carrie ran her hand lazily down Shawn's middle, from her chest through the middle of her breasts, and down her stomach, stopping just above where her legs met. "Oh, I don't know." She produced a large fake yawn. "How tired are you?"

Instead of answering, Shawn softly kissed Carrie's forehead, then pulled Carrie closer. She reached to cup Carrie's face, bringing her lips to hers for a long, lingering kiss.

Carrie sighed. "It's a good thing you're such a good kisser," she whispered against Shawn's lips.

"Why's that?" Shawn asked, in between kisses.

"I'd have given up on you a long time ago," she murmured. "But, my God, you are a good kisser. Like knees buckling good."

"Oh yeah?" Shawn smiled into still another kiss without missing a beat.

"Oh…yeah…"

Shawn pulled Carrie over on top of her as she deepened the kiss, their tongues playing together as they both moaned in response. Shawn pulled away and pushed Carrie into a seated position upon her hips as she pulled Carrie's tank top off over her head, revealing Carrie's bare breasts.

"Oh, God, Carrie…" Shawn moaned as she caressed the silky skin. Carrie leaned forward, giving Shawn's mouth full access to her. As Shawn's tongue toyed with Carrie's nipples and her hands continued fondling the rest of Carrie's breasts, Carrie's breathing quickened and her hips began moving against Shawn's.

Shawn wrapped her arms around Carrie and rolled them both over so Carrie was on her back. She began kissing her way down Carrie's chest and stomach while unbuttoning and removing Carrie's shorts, then her panties. Her lips found their way to that delicate skin inside Carrie's thigh, kissing and running her tongue up her leg, causing Carrie to moan even louder.

As Shawn's mouth met Carrie's center, Carrie whimpered in anticipation. Carrie moved against her and as Shawn's tongue tasted her for the first time, she moaned Shawn's name. Minutes later, when

Carrie reached her peak, Shawn felt her shudder in pleasure. She kissed her way back up Carrie's body, and pulled her over into her arms to hold her close.

She felt Carrie's body relax against her side, Carrie's head settled onto Shawn's shoulder perfectly, and her arm came to rest across Shawn's stomach. Carrie sighed faintly and snuggled in even closer, fitting perfectly in the curve of Shawn's arm around her. She heard Carrie's breathing begin to slow as she fell asleep.

Shawn knew at that moment. She was absolutely sure that Carrie was the one. Not a shred of a doubt remained. She'd always be the one. She was the one she'd wanted all her life. The one that her heart had anticipated but hadn't found until now. She just knew. Kelly was right. She just knew.

CHAPTER THIRTY-SEVEN

SHAWN WOKE UP WITH Carrie still draped across her. She hated to move her, but she really wanted to go check on the weather conditions outside. It was totally dark. She turned on the television for the weather update. They were saying that half of Cape Coral had been evacuated, all the low-lying parts, anyway. Once the storm started, conditions had deteriorated quickly. Everyone needed to be where they were going to be for the duration. She looked back toward the still-sleeping Carrie and knew she was right where she wanted to be. She called Kelly to see how she was doing.

"I'm good," Kelly said. "I'm not in any kind of water flow area or near the river, so I'm pretty sure I'll be just fine. It's kind of boring, though."

"Yeah, I know what you mean. I'm having flashbacks to my childhood, except that my parents kept us busy doing stuff to divert our attention from what was happening."

"Me, too. Growing up here, they just happen. Remember that one year when my family was living in a trailer? That was interesting. Dad had those special tie-downs, I remember that. One hurricane in that thing, though, was enough. It actually rocked some. Mom made a game of it, having us 'camp out' on the floor. We didn't feel it as much there."

"I remember that year. I think that was the year my dad first put me in charge of the hurricane map. You remember those?"

"I sure do. They had them in the newspaper and you could chart where the hurricane was on it in longitude and latitude."

"Right. It wasn't like you couldn't see it on TV anyway, but Dad thought I should do it, too. It was my job during the storm to know where it was at all times. Another way to teach me about maps and to keep me from getting scared at the same time."

"WINK TV had a story on just a while ago about people having hurricane parties. Do you believe people still do stupid stuff like that?

Some people in Fort Myers Beach that are supposed to be evacuated are refusing to leave and having parties instead. They said they thought it wouldn't be as bad as the forecasters are saying, and they were just going to stay up all night and party."

"Wow, I hope they're right. It'd be awful if those people were hurt badly or worse because they didn't leave."

"True. Something could happen at the last minute and it could turn, but it's not looking likely that it will. Oh well, guess we'll just have to wait and see. I hate the waiting part. Did I mention that already?"

"Me, too. Are you planning to stay up all night or sleep through it?"

"Oh, I imagine I'll stay up pretty much all night," Kelly said. "Figure I can sleep tomorrow after it's over. I'll probably doze off and on, but curiosity will get the best of me and I'll check the weather every hour or so. What about you?"

"We took a little nap earlier…don't laugh, we actually did. Carrie's still asleep. I'll probably stay up the rest of the night and do what you're doing. If the power goes off, we've got loads of battery-powered things here, tons of batteries, and can get the weather on a little television or on the radio. We'll be fine."

"Well, stay safe, then. Talk to you later."

"Stay safe yourself." Shawn smiled as she repeated the local hurricane mantra. She picked up the remote and clicked on the Weather Channel again, with the sound on low.

Grace had been upgraded to a category two hurricane, getting stronger and even more organized. That wasn't good, but still they'd be all right. She opened her laptop and began another entry in her hurricane diary. She could hear the palm trees outside rustling in the stiff breeze. *Come on, Grace. Get a move on. Let's get this over with.*

Just after midnight, Shawn woke from hearing Carrie moving around in the kitchen. She could tell it was raining hard from the sound on the metal roof of the front porch. The whole house had a metal roof, but the porch wasn't insulated, making the sound much louder there. She got up and looked out the front door, where she saw the wind had kicked up and was blowing much harder.

They were still getting cable, so they still had television. Forecasters were saying that the eye of the storm was going to pass just to their south, coming ashore near the Everglades. Good for us, she thought, but bad for those poor people down there. Everything down there was even more low-lying than Fort Myers, which was barely above sea level. The winds around the eye were now at one hundred fifteen miles per hour, and what she saw outside was still the outer bands of rain with this huge storm. Grace was finally there.

Shawn opened her laptop, and then plugged it in again to make sure it was fully charged. She wrote: *I'm very tired and may go back to sleep in a while, in spite of my intention to stay up all night. It feels funny to sleep in my clothes, but I feel the need to be dressed. I guess that's a throwback to my childhood. We always slept in our clothes during hurricanes. They never knew what might happen, and it was better to be dressed.*

The people on local television are doing a great job of keeping us informed. I don't think I've ever seen two local networks getting together like this. Channel 2 and Channel 7, ABC and NBC, are working together and staying on all night becoming our own local weather channel. The weather Doppler is showing the big stuff in this huge storm has nearly arrived. Nothing to do here but wait. Wait, wait, and wait. Did I mention I hate waiting?

CHAPTER THIRTY-EIGHT

BY TWO THIRTY MONDAY morning the weather people told them they'd had nearly an inch of rain so far. The power was still on, thank goodness. Looking out the front door, Shawn saw the trees moving around quite a bit, but not alarmingly so. The rain was steady but not heavy. The Doppler image on television showed the eye of the storm was very large, which meant it should be interesting to see what happened when it finally waded ashore.

Shawn realized she was really hungry. She had been ignoring her stomach for some time, but there was no reason to be abusive to it. Since Carrie was dozing on the sofa next to her, Shawn moved slowly so she wouldn't wake her and barefooted into the kitchen to scrounge for a snack. Ah, a ham sandwich, that's what she wanted. She got out the ham, lettuce, tomato, and mustard along with the sourdough bread she had developed a taste for in San Francisco. Nice to see Carrie liked it, too.

As she made her sandwich, she could hear the weather guys on television say that sometime in the next four hours the area would probably lose power for a while. Once again, they were warning people about using a generator inside a building or just outside of a window because of the fumes. She shook her head, wondering how many people were stupid enough to do that, and realized there were always reports after a storm of deaths due to that very thing. Sad to think people would do things intentionally that could kill them, even after all the warnings. But, sadly, some always did.

"Hey, how about making two of those," Carrie said as she padded around the corner into the kitchen, rubbing her eyes.

Shawn reached to put her arms around Carrie and pulled her close for a little kiss. "Hey, I thought you were sleeping."

Carrie snuggled in. "I was, but I woke up hungry and you weren't there, so I figured you were in here for food, too."

"I woke up hungry. What is it about these storms that make you eat more?" She laughed. "I'll make you one. Go sit back down, sweetie, and I'll be there in a minute."

Carrie grinned with sleepy eyes, and headed to the comfort of the sofa while Shawn finished their snack. Outside, the rain was sheeting down. Because it was coming from the south and the house faced north, the front porch was still mostly dry so far. They could hear the rain hammering on the house roof now, as well as the porch roof and the shutters on the windows around the house. The eye wall of the storm was nearly at landfall to the south.

After handing Carrie her sandwich, Shawn munched on hers as she headed to the door to look outside yet again. "Have you seen this? We haven't hit the worst of it yet, but those poor trees out by the road are really swishing around. Can't see much, but you can sure hear them."

"You know, those trees have been there for what seems like forever. They even went through Charlie. Don't worry." Carrie nodded toward the television. "While you were in the kitchen, they said we'll experience the heaviest winds in the next few hours as Grace comes ashore. They're still saying near Everglades City. Ever been there?"

Shawn came back to sit on the sofa and put her arm around Carrie, who snuggled up next to her. She knew Carrie was trying to distract her from the storm. "Just when I was a kid. Seems like we went down there once for airboat rides. I don't remember much about it except for how loud that boat ride was. I seem to remember it being a ways south of Naples."

"Yes, a bit, about twenty miles or so. I was only there once a long time ago. I drove down with a friend whose dad was pastor of a church there. It was a tiny town in the middle of nowhere, really, but kind of a neat place. Old Florida, if you know what I mean. Unfortunately, it was summer when we visited and the mosquitoes just about ate us alive. You had to go out after dusk when the mosquitoes seemed to go to sleep or something. During the day it was just awful." She rubbed her arms, remembering. "I can't imagine those people bearing the brunt of that storm. It's totally flat. Just barely dry land."

"No, I can't either. I'm grateful Grace decided to go somewhere else to come ashore, but feel awful for them. Just the storm surge alone will cause some major damage there."

Shawn got up and turned on the little battery-powered television, tuned it to the correct channel and then turned it off. "Just to be ready." She did the same to the battery-powered radio.

"Are you getting nervous? How long has it been since you went through a hurricane?"

"A long time." Shawn thought for a minute. "I'm not sure how long. I wasn't here for Agatha. I was gone. The house was all closed up, so I didn't worry too much about it. I just had someone come over to see if it was intact afterward, and that was all. Probably the last time I was actually in a hurricane, not just the rain bands, but the hurricane itself, was when I was a kid."

Carrie put her arms around Shawn. "You know we're safe. Whatever happens, we'll be fine. We may have to do some cleanup afterward, maybe put up with some power outage, but we're ready and everything will be okay."

Shawn relaxed into Carrie's arms. It was so nice to feel someone taking care of her a bit. Someone who actually cared about her. She looked into Carrie's eyes and saw a calm there from the storm.

CHAPTER THIRTY-NINE

CARRIE WOKE AT FIVE thirty a.m., wrapped in Shawn's arms on the living room sofa. Shawn's heart beat in her right ear, with the sound of rain pouring down outside in the other. She sighed and snuggled in more. In spite of the hour, it was still quite dark outside from what she could see through the front door. The local television weather guy was saying that the winds were up to sixty-eight miles per hour and the rain total up to five inches, which was fairly normal for a storm of this kind. The eye of the storm was aground around Marco Island and Everglades City. The announcer was saying there were power outages around Fort Myers, but obviously, it had not happened to them yet.

She got up to get a better look out the front door and could see the palm trees whipping around in the wind gusts, but she didn't see any tree limbs down other than some palm fronds when she shined a flashlight into the yard. The rain seemed to be coming down sideways for a bit, and then back to normal. The gusts had to be heavy to cause that.

As she stood there she realized that on a regular day just about now she'd be in the shower, getting ready for work. Speaking of, she decided it was time to make some coffee while the power was still on. As she headed to the kitchen, she passed Shawn still dozing on the sofa and couldn't help lightly caressing her blonde waves.

By the time Carrie had put the coffee on and returned to the sofa, Shawn was awake. "They just said there'll be a ten p.m. curfew starting tonight," she said as Carrie nestled back into the sofa.

"Well, we weren't planning on going out tonight anyway, right? Or do you have some hot date you didn't tell me about?"

"Oh, I've got a hot date, all right." Shawn teased back, grinning. "But she's right here." Shawn wrapped her arms around Carrie. Carrie leaned into those arms as Shawn's lips nuzzled her neck just below her ear, giving her goosebumps all over her body.

"Are you cold?"

"Nope, just the opposite, actually. You just went for my second most sensitive spot."

"Oh yeah? And remind me where the first was?" Shawn laughed, her hand stroking slowly downward on Carrie's belly.

"Mmm...nice. Maybe we should save that for a bit, though. Coffee's probably ready and I'm thinking maybe we should eat something hot while we can. How about I make us some breakfast?"

"Eating. My second most favorite thing to do that doesn't include writing."

"Oh, really. And what's the first?" Carrie swished dramatically into the kitchen.

Shawn gave her a look that said she knew that Carrie knew the answer to that question. By the time Carrie had their breakfast ready, the sun appeared to be finally coming up, but it was just barely light outside. As they ate their bacon and scrambled eggs, they could hear the rain coming down harder, being blown by the wind that had also kicked up another notch.

Twice while they were eating, Shawn got up to look outside. Although the television was on, giving them blow-by-blow information about the storm situation, there was nothing quite the same as looking out the front door window. Since it was recessed under the deep front porch, it was somewhat protected. Still, some of the rain was hitting the now-empty front porch and the front door.

"The rain and wind seem to be coming from everywhere at once. The palm trees seem to be doing some kind of wild dance, waving their arms around in odd circles."

"No one but a writer would come up with that description," Carrie said, joining Shawn at the window. "But it definitely fits."

"Maybe they're waving their arms around trying to get the storm to stop, almost like they've had enough."

Carrie laughed. "Yep, that fits, too."

When they returned to the living room, they could hear the television guy saying the winds were shifting around to come from the northeast. That explained the winds appearing to be moving around in a circle. Just then, the cable went out, along with the power.

"Oh boy, there it goes," Carrie said. "So much for..." Before she could say anything else, they both came back on again. Knowing this was going to happen again soon, they began checking everything around the house and filled one more jug of water to stick in the freezer.

"So much for showers for the duration," Shawn said. "Looks like it's a good thing I was clean before this started." Shawn laughed.

"Very clean," Carrie said suggestively.

Shawn grabbed her around the waist, picked her up and carried her to the bed, dropping her there. She pinned Carrie to the bed and kissed her soundly. Before anything else could happen, though, they heard a loud crash that sounded like it came from out in front of the house. They both jumped up and ran to the front door. The sight greeting them there was the huge tree that had been next to Carrie's driveway, lying across the road, its roots in the air.

"Oh, no...not that tree." Carrie's eyes filled up.

Shawn put her arm around Carrie and pulled her close. "I'm so sorry."

"My granddad planted that tree when they bought this place as a young couple. My mom had a swing in it. I climbed it as a kid, too. So many memories are tied up with that tree. It made it through so many storms, I can't believe this one brought it down."

"Well, not to make light of this, but there is a good thing about this: it didn't fall on anyone or anything. Well, except the road, and it's mostly limbs in the road. It'll take time to cut it up to get it out of there, though. Good thing there's another way in and out of here."

"I guess that's true. But I'll miss it. Now it'll wind up as firewood." Carrie wiped her eyes with part of her tank top.

"Firewood to warm someone's evening in winter. Or maybe someone will build something out of part of it and use it in their home. Your tree could have another life somewhere making someone else happy."

"True. I guess you're right." Carrie wiped her eyes again. "We should tell Kelly about this after the storm is over. She likes to build things. Maybe she could get some of it and build something nice. That'd be a great thing to happen to my tree."

"Good idea. Maybe she can get here before the emergency crews come take it away."

Just then, the power and cable went out completely. They waited for a few minutes, then realized it was out for good. Since they had plenty of batteries, they turned on the little battery-powered television. The weather guy was still on, talking about more power outages. They said those without power would be out until at least the next day, while Florida Power and Light or Lee County Electric Co-op took care of emergencies first.

Carrie moved one of the frozen water jugs to the refrigerator, which had just effectively become a large cooler. There wasn't much left that needed to be kept cold, but at least there'd be some cool water to drink later.

When Carrie returned to the living room, Shawn said, "They just said the tropical force winds should be done in another hour or two. It shouldn't be much longer after that when we can go out and look around. I'm sure my house is just fine, but I'd like to see for myself."

"I don't blame you for that. We can also get the generator started up and we can run the fans and the TV off that, and of course the coffee maker. Batteries only last so long."

"Wonderful. We should be good for the couple of days it might take to get the power back on."

CHAPTER FORTY

AS THE MORNING BECAME early afternoon, the rain slacked off and then the winds began backing off as well. It was beginning to look like just another breezy day as the sun came out finally and the sky cleared up. Carrie and Shawn were happy to see that the water stayed on. The bad news was that lots of areas were now under a boil order, meaning don't drink any of it unless you boil it first. The good thing was that they had plenty of stored "good" water.

Shawn and Carrie walked around Carrie's house to check for damage. Except for a small tear in the porch screen, a lot of palm fronds, and some smaller tree limbs littering her yard and roof, there was no real damage except for the demise of Carrie's big tree.

They walked around the downed tree and the large hole in the ground the roots left behind. Carrie took Shawn's hand and held it tight as she ran her other hand along the tree's trunk and patted it like an old friend. She brushed away another couple of tears, then looked at Shawn. "Let's call Kelly. We need to check on her anyway and let's ask her if she can salvage some wood for some good use."

"Okay," Shawn said, pulling Carrie's hand up to place a small kiss on her fingers. She dropped Carrie's hand and put her arm around her as they stood there looking at the arboreal corpse, with its root feet stuck up in the air. She didn't mention this image to Carrie. She didn't think she'd consider that image amusing right then.

"Kelly, I see you're still alive," Shawn said when Kelly answered.

"Alive and kicking. You guys have power?"

"Nope. Lost it a bit ago. How about you?"

"I have power here now. It was off for a little bit, but I saw on the news that lots of people are still out. I think I'm in the part of town on the same grid as the hospital, so ours would be back on first, anyway. At least that's the rumor around here. You guys good over there?"

"We're fine except for one thing. Carrie lost that big tree that was in front of her house. It fell across the yard and into the street here."

"Oh, no. That's too bad. It was a beautiful old tree."

Shawn looked over at Carrie. "Yes, it was. That tree meant a lot to her. She wants to know if you'd like to come over and get some of the wood before the emergency crews take it."

"I'd love to," Kelly said. "I actually do own a chain saw, believe it or not. Want me to bring you guys anything? Besides myself and my chainsaw, that is."

"I can't think of anything, but hold on. Putting you on speaker." Shawn looked at Carrie. "Kelly wants to know if we want her to bring us anything." Carrie nodded no. "Nope, we're good. Oh, on second thought, could you bring us a bag of ice, if you can get it. We'll get the generator working and make some margaritas. How does that sound?"

"That sounds great. Carrie, I'm so sorry about your tree. I'd love to come get some wood from it. I'll hunt down some ice and see you in a bit. A nice cold margarita sounds wonderful right now. I'll call you when I'm on my way."

Shawn and Carrie walked around the tree and headed down the street to Shawn's house. It looked intact, no pieces of roof missing or even ripped screen on the porch. Those old metal screens were tough. But there were plenty of palm fronds all over the yard. Fortunately, that's all there was. No other downed trees.

Shawn unlocked her front door and they went inside to make sure everything was still secure. They opened a window to let in some air, since a little would come in even under the storm shutters. In the darkened house, Shawn was happy to see that everything appeared just as she left it—nothing broken anything. Without thinking, she flipped a light switch in the kitchen then felt silly when nothing happened. They'd have to go through her refrigerator in a bit and toss out things that would be bad, but that could wait for a little while.

Carrie followed her as they walked into Shawn's new bedroom. "You haven't been in here before, have you?" Shawn asked. "Well, we'll fix that right now."

Shawn took Carrie's hand and led her around the room, pointing out the white wicker bed and dresser. Then she showed her the new master bathroom, with its blue and white tiles. Back in the bedroom, Shawn steered Carrie over to her bed and gave her a little push to sit her down onto it. "There. Now you've been on my bed." She laughed and pulled Carrie down with her, lying across the bed. "You don't know how many times I pictured you here with me."

"And you've no idea how many times I tried to picture you with me. It took us long enough, didn't it?" Their lips touched in a soft, sweet kiss. "We'd better stop fooling around, though. Kelly's coming."

A few minutes later as they wandered around outside, checking the back yard, Shawn pulled her close and kissed Carrie softly, and then continued walking holding her hand.

"What was that for?" Carrie asked her.

"That was for just you being you and being here with me. I really appreciate you."

"Well, thanks, but that's what people do for each other. Especially if they care about each other. And I do care about you."

Shawn stopped, turned to Carrie and took Carrie's hands in hers. She brought Carrie's hands to her lips and kissed the backs of both hands tenderly. She continued to look at Carrie's hands in hers for a bit longer before looking up into those brown eyes that entranced her.

"Carrie, I more than care about you. I love you." Shawn kept looking into her eyes, waiting for a response.

Carrie slowly smiled, pulled Shawn close, and whispered in her ear, "I love you, too." Their lips met in a sweet kiss as they held each other briefly.

"Thank goodness!" Shawn said when she let go of Carrie. "Then you did forgive me?"

Carrie giggled, causing her to wonder what she was thinking. "Sweetie, I forgive you for what you did. Let's pretend what happened never did. This is a new beginning for us."

"It Is. We go from here on together. How 'bout that?"

"I love the sound of that. Now let's get the generator started and see if you can make us some margaritas. Then we'll have the rest of that chocolate pie."

CHAPTER FORTY-ONE

DECEMBER IN FLORIDA IS warm in the daytime and cool at night. On a somewhat chilly late Saturday afternoon, Carrie's phone rang. "Are you home? I have something for you," Kelly said. "I'd like to bring it over in just a bit if that's all right."

"Sure, we're here putting up the tree. Why don't you plan on staying for supper, unless you have something else going on? I'm making one of Shawn's favorites, country fried steak."

"With mashed potatoes and gravy?"

"Of course."

"And biscuits!" Shawn chimed in from a few feet away.

"You just talked me into it. I'd love to."

Twenty minutes later, Carrie and Shawn saw Kelly's blue Durango pulling into the driveway. A text message on Shawn's phone said for Carrie to not look out the front windows and to please cover her eyes until she gave the okay. Carrie laughed at the theatrics, but complied. She sat on the sofa and closed her eyes and put her hands over them for good measure.

Shawn left Carrie on the sofa and went out to see what Kelly was up to. By then, Kelly had the hatch open on the cargo area. When Kelly stepped aside and let Shawn look in, she just stood there, staring, for a few seconds.

Carrie couldn't really hear much of anything from inside the house, but she didn't want to spoil the surprise by peeking. She kept her eyes closed even when she could hear Shawn and Kelly opening and closing doors. Then she heard a bit of a thunk sound. Still, she waited.

"Okay, open your eyes," Kelly said.

She opened her eyes and stood up. Her mouth dropped open and both of her hands reached to her cheeks. "Oh. My. God."

There in front of her was a beautifully crafted rocking chair. The wood was expertly fitted together and warmly stained. She reached to touch it. It felt like silk under her hands.

"Go ahead, sit in it," Kelly urged. "I made it from the wood I took from your grandfather's tree."

Carrie couldn't seem to find any words. She turned around and sat down. It fit her perfectly. The chair and its arms seemed to wrap themselves around her like a hug. Tears welled up and began spilling down her cheeks. She made no attempt to brush them away.

Kelly crouched down in front of her. "Oh, no. I didn't mean to make you cry. Are you all right?"

Carrie reached for Kelly and hugged her hard, her tears wetting Kelly's shirt. "It's wonderful. It's perfect, just perfect. I can never thank you enough for it."

Kelly hugged her back. "I'm just glad you like it. It was my pleasure to do this for you."

Carrie finally released Kelly and rocked slowly in the chair. Shawn handed her a tissue to sop up the residual tears from her face. "How did you come up with the idea of a rocking chair, Kelly? You couldn't have known I've always wanted one. I don't think I've even told Shawn, so she couldn't have told you."

"I tried to think of something you didn't have, but something you could enjoy not only using, but looking at as well. I considered a table or something else along those lines, but I kept coming back to a rocking chair. Then I came up with this design. The curving arms sort of cuddle you when you sit in it. I thought you might find it comforting when you're missing your grandparents or don't feel good. I thought it might also make a nice place to sit and read. I tried to make it look pretty for you, so you'd enjoy looking at the wood as well."

"Oh, Kelly, you did a wonderful job on it." Carrie stood up and stepped away from the rocker. "Shawn, come here and sit in it. Isn't it amazing?"

Shawn had been standing back. This was Kelly's moment, after all. She stroked the wood in the back of the chair, the smooth contours begging to be touched. She ran her hand down the slats in the back, and then along both of the curved arms as she sat down.

"Kelly, it truly is amazing. I knew you were talented, but this...this is such a piece of art."

Kelly stood there, grinning from ear to ear. "I'm so glad you both like it. Once I understood the story of that tree, I knew I had to make something meaningful out of it. This was truly a labor of love. I felt your grandfather would have wanted you to have something like this to remember him by. That's how I thought of it, as a present from him."

Carrie felt the tears begin again and put her arms around Kelly. "I'm so grateful to you. I had no idea you would do something this elaborate or wonderful. You are such a dear friend, and I will always love you for doing this for me."

"You're welcome. Believe me, this was my pleasure. But there's something else." Kelly stepped away from Carrie and looked at both of them. "Wait just a minute, I'll be right back," she said as she headed for the door.

"What in the world could she be up to now?" Shawn got up from the rocker and put her arm around Carrie as they watched Kelly go out to the passenger side of the Durango and remove a box wrapped in paper with a big ribbon.

"I know you two are meant for each other," Kelly said as she handed the box to Shawn. "This is for both of you. It's your first Christmas together, the first of many to come. You don't have to wait to open it, though."

"Before we open it, there's something we want to tell you." Shawn put her arm back around Carrie, who smiled back and nodded. "You're the first to know. We're getting married this coming spring."

Kelly's face lit up as she reached for both of them in a group hug, practically lifting both of them off the floor. "Oh. My. God. I'm so happy for the two of you! If any two people belong together, it's you two. Well, then, consider this your engagement present. Open it."

Shawn handed the box to Carrie and proceeded to untie the ribbon and take the pretty paper off the box.

"Oh, for crying out loud, will you get to it? You haven't changed a bit, have you? You're still taking forever to open anything. Be forewarned, Carrie, this is what you'll have to live with."

They all laughed as Shawn finally got the box opened and pushed aside the paper covering the object inside. Shawn and Carrie both gasped when they realized what they were looking at. They took it out and stared.

A wooden box. Another exquisite piece of woodworking. It appeared to be about twelve inches long by eight inches wide and six inches tall. There were two initials carved into the lid: S and C, intertwined. The box had been pieced together so perfectly, it was as if the wood grew into that shape naturally with all those different colors.

"It's so beautiful," Carrie said softly. "Just. Wow."

"It's a treasure box," Kelly explained. "You can put things in it that remind the two of you of things you've done together, places you've seen. You know, like ticket stubs, tiny sea shells, things like that. Better than a scrapbook, because you can handle the things again."

Shawn and Carrie each hugged Kelly again.

"Oh, I forgot to tell you something," Kelly said. "There's something special about this box."

"Beside the fact that you made it, you mean?" Shawn said.

Kelly grinned. "Yes, beside that. Part of the wood in this box came from Carrie's tree, but another part of it came from a tree in Shawn's yard."

"Really? What a great idea. How'd you come up with it?" Shawn said.

Kelly grinned and continued, "It's a combination of the two, like the love you have for each other. I had that bit of leftover wood from Carrie's tree, and when I started thinking about it, the idea just came to me."

"You never cease to amaze me," Shawn said. "I might have to steal this idea for my next novel."

"Steal away. The treasure box is yours. Now, what was this I heard about country fried steak?"

CHAPTER FORTY-TWO

SPRING. THE FOLLOWING YEAR. A private beach on Sanibel Island near sunset. A warm breeze wafted off the Gulf of Mexico, lightly ruffling the white gauze draped over a small gazebo on the sand. Carrie and Shawn walked hand in hand, coming down the beach. Carrie's loose hair and long lavender halter dress moved with the breeze. Shawn was absolutely sure she had never seen anyone look more beautiful. Her own lavender shirt and white pants had been selected to coordinate with Carrie's dress.

As they approached the gazebo, they waved to the group gathered there and the minister welcomed them. Kelly stood in front, with Greg, AJ, Rich and his wife, and other friends, as well as Carrie's mom, waiting for them. Shawn looked over at Carrie and squeezed her hand before pressing Carrie's fingers to her lips for a soft kiss.

Carrie looked into Shawn's eyes and mouthed, "I love you, honey." Shawn smiled, her heart full almost to bursting looking at the love of her life. "I love you, too," she mouthed back.

Turning toward the gazebo, facing the minister, they gazed out over the Gulf of Mexico as the sun began to set. The swishing of waves breaking gently onto the sugar sand was all the music needed as Kelly lit two torches, one on each side of the gazebo. The minister had been holding the treasure box Kelly made for them. She held the box out to them now, and Shawn and Carrie each placed a small shell into it, and then they closed it and handed the box to Kelly to hold.

The minister began the ceremony. "We are gathered here today to celebrate the marriage of Shawn and Carrie. By your presence, you celebrate with them the love they have discovered in each other and, by being here you support their decision to commit themselves to one another for the rest of their lives. The greatest happiness of life is the conviction that we are loved, loved for ourselves. If there is anything better than being loved it is loving. Today we are here to celebrate love.

We come together to witness and proclaim the joining of these two persons in marriage. This is the union of two individuals in heart, body, mind, and spirit. Therefore, a marriage is not to be entered into lightly, but reverently, honestly, and deliberately. It is into this union that Shawn and Carrie come now to be joined."

Shawn looked over and winked at Carrie causing her to blush.

"Remember always that love, loyalty, and trust are the foundations of a lasting and happy union. As you strive to fulfill the commitment that you declare to one another here, your life together can be increasingly full of joy, satisfaction, and peace. I pray that you will hold fast to the vision and the promise of this special day. A Native American marriage poem puts it this way:

Now you will feel no rain,

For each of you will be shelter for each other.

Now you will feel no cold,

For each of you will be warmth for the other.

Now there will be no loneliness,

For each of you will be companion to the other.

Now you are two bodies,

But there is only one life before you.

Treat yourselves and each other with respect, reminding yourselves often of what brought you together. Give the highest priority to the tenderness, gentleness, and kindness that your connection deserves. When frustration, difficulty, and fear assail your relationship, as they threaten all relationships at one time or another, remember to focus on what is right between you, not only the part which seems wrong. In this way you can ride out the storms when clouds hide the face of the sun in your lives, remembering that even if you lose sight of it for a moment, the sun is still there. If each of you takes responsibility for the quality of your life together, it will be marked by abundance and delight."

"Please face each other and join both hands." The minister touched Shawn's shoulder briefly. "Shawn, what would you like to say to Carrie?"

Shawn swallowed hard and looked into Carrie's eyes, her knees nearly buckling. "Carrie, you have shown me what real love is. I love you with all my heart and soul, and will spend the rest of my life showing you that you are cherished. I promise to always love and respect you and never give you a reason to doubt my love. I promise to be your lover, companion and friend, ally in conflict, and your student and teacher. I promise to be your comrade in adventure, consolation in disappointment, accomplice in mischief, and your strength in need. I promise to be open and honest with you, to share my life and worldly possessions, my thoughts and feelings. I pledge to stand by and respect you, to rejoice in your growth and always show you honesty and love."

The minister briefly touched Carrie's shoulder. "Carrie, what would you like to say to Shawn?"

Carrie looked down at Shawn's hands, still holding hers, and then into Shawn's eyes. "Shawn, I thought I knew what I was looking for in a partner. I was holding out for that romantic ideal I read about in stories. Little did I know you would actually walk into my life as far more than I could ever have dreamed. I love you with all my heart and soul, and will spend the rest of my life making sure you know you are cherished. I promise to love and respect you and make sure you never have a reason to doubt my love. I promise to be your lover, companion, and friend, ally in conflict, and your student and teacher. I promise to be your comrade in adventure, consolation in disappointment, accomplice in mischief, and your strength in need. I promise to be open and honest with you, to share my life and worldly possessions, my thoughts and feelings. I pledge to stand by and respect you, to rejoice in your growth, and always show you honesty and love."

"Shawn and Carrie, we now come to your marriage vows. I remind you that saying your vows to each other is one thing but nothing is more challenging than living them day-by-day. What you promise today must be renewed tomorrow and every day that stretches out before you."

Shawn felt her stomach clench, and then smiled it away. She knew this was what she wanted with Carrie. This was what she had dreamed of from the time they became lovers. Gazing into Carrie's eyes, she could see the love reflected there, and felt whole. She swallowed hard. "I, Shawn, take you, Carrie, to be my beloved partner in life. I will stand behind, beside, and with you always, in times of celebration and in times of sorrow, in times of joy and in times of pain, in times of sickness and in times of health. I will live with you, love and cherish you as long as we both shall live."

She saw the smile on Carrie's lips as she repeated the same words back to her, then squeezed both her hands briefly.

The minister asked, "May I have the rings please?"

Kelly handed over the simple matching gold bands, then the minister continued.

"Now we will have the blessing of the rings: May these rings be blessed as the symbol of this affectionate unity. These two lives are now joined in one unbroken circle. Wherever they go, they will always return to one another in their togetherness. These two find in each other the love for which all men and women yearn, promising to grow in understanding and in compassion. The home they establish together will be such a place of sanctuary that many will find there a friend. These rings, on their fingers, symbolize the touch of the Spirit of Love in their hearts. Shawn, please place this ring on Carrie's finger and repeat after me."

Shawn's hand trembled slightly as she placed the band on Carrie's ring finger. She was suddenly grateful she hadn't had to memorize these vows. Her mind went blank as she looked into the face of her forever love. In the deepening dusk, torchlights dancing in the Gulf breeze, she said, "I give you this ring as a symbol of my love and faithfulness. As I place it on your finger, I commit my heart and soul to you. As it encircles your finger, may it remind you always that you are surrounded by my enduring love. I pledge you my love, my respect, my laughter and my tears. With all that I am, I honor you."

Carrie slid an identical gold band onto Shawn's finger. "I give you this ring as a symbol of my love and faithfulness. As I place it on your finger, I commit my heart and soul to you. As it encircles your finger, may it remind you always that you are surrounded by my enduring love." She paused and looked at the ring she had just placed on Shawn's finger, a little tear forming in the corner of her eye and finding its way down her cheek, followed by another. Her voice trembled as she continued, "I pledge you my love, my respect, my laughter and my tears. With all that I am, I honor you."

Shawn squeezed Carrie's hand, tears forming in her eyes as well. She reached over to gently wipe Carrie's tears with her thumb and she blinked her own away as the minister continued.

"Now may those who wear these rings live in love all their days. May the love which has brought you together continue to grow and enrich your lives. May you continue to meet with courage the problems which may arise to challenge you. May your marriage always be one of love and trust. May the happiness you share today be with you always, and may everything you have said and done here today become a living truth in your lives.

"Shawn and Carrie, we have heard your promise to share your lives in matrimony. We recognize and respect the covenant you have made here this day before each one of us as witnesses. Therefore in honesty and sincerity of what you have said and done here today, and by the power vested in me by the State of Florida, it is now my personal privilege and great joy to be the first to introduce Shawn and Carrie as partners in life...for life...wife and wife...spouse and spouse. May beauty surround you both on the journey ahead and through all the years, and may happiness be your companion always. Go now to enter into the days of your life together, and may your days be good and long upon the earth. You may kiss your spouse."

Shawn grinned and looked into Carrie's eyes, wrapped her in her arms, and kissed her wife for the first of many times to come.

The End

ABOUT BJ PHILLIPS

I've been writing practically since I've been reading. People who knew me well knew my biggest dream and biggest fear was writing a whole book. That fear of failure. I had poetry published in my school literary magazine and a funny story in my work professional magazine. I wrote training materials for work and helped friends write their resumes, feeling that was at least writing. I had the beginnings of fantasy stories, mysteries, and love stories all sitting in folders and notebooks.

In the summer of 2013 I saw the National Novel Writing Month (NaNoWriMo) challenge. If you're not familiar with it, the challenge is to write 50,000 words in 30 days. The day after Thanksgiving that year, I posted 51,000 words and a complete story was born. It needed a lot of work, but it was there. That story was the bones of Hurricane Season, my debut novel, which will be out in spring 2016.

Early in 2014, I heard about a new program through the Golden Crown Literary Society (GCLS) called the Writing Academy. It's a one year program aimed at new writers or writers who want to improve their skills. I'm proud to be part of the very first graduating class.
The Writing Academy was life-changing. I started looking at myself as an author, not just as someone who happens to write. I retired the beginning of 2015. I became a full time writer of stories and finally finished my first book the end of July, 2015.

I live in Florida with my partner, a retired police officer, Maya the Yorkie, and Piper the Chihuahua in an honest-to-goodness resort—it says so on the sign out front. When I'm not writing, we love sitting out on the front porch with the "kids" and chatting with neighbors and friends who like to come by and visit. I'm an avid reader of anything that strikes my fancy and I love puzzles – like logic problems, Sudoku or word finds. I also like to take walks, go to flea markets, sketch, and crochet. Okay, I'm also addicted to several TV shows, mostly mysteries and cop shows. Thank goodness for the DVR!

I'm very excited about becoming part of the Desert Palm Press family. I have two more books in the pipeline right now, a murder mystery and another romance.

Connect with BJ

Email: bjphillipswrites@gmail.com

Website: www.bjphillipsauthor.com

Twitter: https//twitter.com/bjwrites01

More Romance from Desert Palm Press

AJ Adaire
Sunset Island
ISBN: 9781301136629

Ren Madison is certain her life couldn't be more perfect. She owns a private island with an Inn off the coast of Maine. She treasures her loving relationship with her older brother Jack, his wife, Marie, and dotes on her niece Laura. She has a passionate and supportive relationship with her partner, Brooke, and a successful business that doesn't require her undivided attention allowing her ample time to pursue her true passion, painting.

Ren's idyllic world crumbles when Brooke dies. Friends and family worry that Ren may never fully recover from her loss.

Dr. Lindy Caprini, a multi-lingual professor, is looking for an artist to illustrate the book she is writing comparing fairy tales from around the world. To make working together on the book easier, Lindy takes a year sabbatical and leaves friends, home, and boyfriend in Pennsylvania and moves to Ren's island. Ren soon discovers that the beautiful and mischievous Lindy is a talented author and a witty conversationalist. Their collaboration on the book leads to a close, light hearted, and flirtatious friendship. Will their collaboration end there?

The Interim (a novelette)
ISBN: 9781311099051

Devastated that her partner cheated, Melanie flees to a new job in Maine, where she meets Ren Madison. Ren is dealing with issues of her own after losing her partner Brooke in a plane crash

What happens in the interim after one relationship ends and you're really ready to love again? For Ren Madison, Melanie was what happened.

The Interim fills in the details of Ren Madison's life on Sunset Island after Brooke but before Lindy.

Awaiting My Assignment
ISBN: 9781310825248

Bernie was a liar. Amanda learned that much when she caught her lover cheating the first time. Upon discovering a second indiscretion,

Amanda vows there will never be another. She leaves the relationship, fleeing to her friend Dana in New York State. While staying at Dana's home, Amanda meets and falls in love with a wonderful woman named Mallory.

Amanda is ready to move on. However, the consistently surprising Bernie isn't finished yet. Amanda learns of Bernie's rudest betrayal yet when she receives a package from her recently deceased ex-lover. A very surprising revelation and one final request are contained therein. The favor comes with a gift that delivers dramatic and life-altering changes, not only to Amanda's life, but to the lives of her closest friends and new partner as well.

Anything Your Heart Desires
ISBN: 978131163912

"Whoa—lesbians!" That was Stacy Alexander's first thought as she observes the group of women in the new shop across the street kiss each other in greeting. Stacy had been staring out her apartment window trying to think of a motive for the death of the character she'd killed off in her mystery novel. Ah ha—extortion! What could be a better reason for the murder of my heroine than being blackmailed because she's a lesbian? Now all I need is a lesbian to teach me about the 'lesbian lifestyle.'

That's where policewoman Jo Martin enters the picture. Jo has two rules by which she religiously lives her life: never get involved with someone already in a relationship and never, ever date a straight woman. As Jo and Stacy collaborate on the novel, will Stacy want to gain a more intimate knowledge of the topic, and will Jo hold steadfastly to her rules?

Desert Palm Press

One Day Longer Than Forever
ISBN: 9781310847738

Dr. Kate Martin needs a vacation after a failed romance with her business partner nearly ruins her. Lee Foster is recovering from her first lesbian relationship that self-destructed when her partner moved several states away, leaving her behind.

Two failed romances, a double booked vacation cabin, and a blizzard—will fate intervene again and turn a passionate affair with a stranger, into something more?

Desert Palm Press

It's Complicated
ISBN: 9781311122964

Victoria Brannigham had a guilty pleasure. Every day she would take a detour, sit on the boardwalk, and wait. She tried not to covet what could never be hers. Beverly McMannis was lonely, until she discovered another lesbian on the island. Bev eagerly embraced the growing friendship with her neighbor. Victoria was honest with Bev right from the start; explaining that she wasn't free to explore their attraction. Bev promised to honor the boundaries. Love isn't always easy, sometimes it's complicated...especially when she doesn't know you're still being faithful.

Desert Palm Press

I Love My Life
ISBN: 9781311310002

Betrayal by her former partner sends Chris Baxter fleeing to Maine. To escape the monotony of staring at the four walls of her isolated cabin, she enrolls in a sailing class. A chance pairing with Stephanie Kincaid and her cohorts, Tina and Terry, offers an opportunity for new friendship. Their shared homework assignment might offer Chris the potential for more than just knowledge of navigation.

An urgent message interrupts the classmates' sailing vacation along the coast of Maine. While Chris rushes back to her twin's bedside, the others remain onboard to sail back to their homeport. Will the revelations from her ex, her sister, and her family, change everything in the new life that Chris has rebuilt?

Journey To You
ISBN: 9781311571854

What do you do if you are one of the few who remain alive after a mysterious, flu-like virus claims most of the global population? This is a question Kim Robins and Peri Henderson have to answer when the world changes and society falls apart.

Violent gangs of looters make it unsafe to remain in the city. Hoping to improve their chances for survival, Kim and Peri decide to hike into the remote forest area of Maine.

Dangerous circumstances along the trail cause the women to join forces with another hiker and her dog. The longtime friends and their new companions set off on a daunting trek filled with both menacing and kindhearted survivors.

In this romantic adventure, the real question to be answered is, will this journey bring each of the women the happiness and safety she seeks?

S.L. Kassidy
Please Baby
ISBN: 9781311485137

Jayce Newton's life is going downhill after she rescues her little niece from an awful situation. She plans to hold onto her niece and gain custody of her, but there are some factors against her. Her girlfriend doesn't want the baby around. Her mother wants to take the baby from her, and her brother has disappeared. Things only seem to get worse when Gus Tucker comes into her life.

Gus Tucker's life isn't going much better. She recently divorced her wife and moved into a new home. She's looking forward to a new start and spending time with her sister. Before she can do that, though, she ends up causing trouble for Jayce Newton, getting her fired from her job and kicked out of her home. She tries to make it up to Jayce by taking her in during her time of need. Now, it's just a struggle to see if they're able to coexist in the same house with a baby between them.

Desert Palm Press

Scarred Series
Scarred for Life
ISBN: 9781310171352
Dane Wolfe is a loner. Forsaken by her family and betrayed by people close to her, she has lost all faith in people and spends her days wandering the streets with no direction or meaning. She drifts through life, existing and nothing more. Nicole Cardell is a successful attorney. She has too much faith in people and is being taken advantage of by her boyfriend, Tyler, Dane's cousin. She's tired of his selfish ways and tosses him out. The bad relationship leaves her questioning her judgment. Circumstances bring Dane and Nicole together and a friendship brings them closer. They're able to heal each other and bring balance to each other's lives. Their peace is shattered when family causes trouble and tears them apart. Will they find their path back to each other and to the love that was slowly growing?

New Cuts, Old Wounds
ISBN: 9781310217289
In this sequel to *Scarred for Life*, Nicole Cardell and Dane Wolfe have been together for a year. They are doing their best to move forward with their relationship and open up to each other. It's time to meet family members. Dane's nervous about meeting Nicole's family, but she's even more nervous about Nicole meeting her family. Nicole is eager for both. Nicole thinks Dane should bond with her family while Dane thinks she needs to get as far away from them as possible. The Wolfe family seems to agree with Dane, but keep inviting her to things and Nicole keeps accepting the invites. Will family make or break Dane and Nicole?

Bandages
ISBN: 9781942976103

Life is good for Dane and Nicole. The musician gave the lawyer a ring, a not-engagement ring, a promise; this is forever. But, they both still had some growing and healing to work through.

Healing is strange. There are those days when the bandage falls off on its own and you think you're good to go. Days when laughter comes easy and you forget the past. And there are days when the past doesn't want to be forgotten; you still need a stitch or a cast to hold yourself together. There are even relapses when the poisonous past needs release. Share their journey through eighteen short stories of play, passion, and a deepening partnership. You'll enjoy the journey as much as where it leads.

Desert Palm Press

TJ Whittle
Without Your Courage
ISBN: 9781310147548

What does courage look like to you? Is it a young girl facing an unwanted marriage? Does it echo the fears of a spouse exposing their secret? Is it the strength of a young woman protecting her unborn child? Perhaps it's as simple as a first kiss. Without Your Courage takes us to Auckland, New Zealand and the surrounding countryside, to join the lives of four strong women. 1940s. Violet and Charlotte form a beautiful friendship while John is away at war. What will happen when he returns? Present Day. An accident introduces Ella and Gemma, who struggle to define their new friendship across the barrier of age. Four women with their lives entwined. Will they find the love they seek?

Desert Palm Press

Note to Readers:

We have made every effort to edit this book. However, typos do slip in. If you find an error in the text, please email lee@desertpalmpress.com so the issue can be corrected. We appreciate you as a reader and want to ensure you enjoy the reading process.

Bright blessing.